"Women like you ought to be locked away!"

Kathryn was startled as much by the grimness of Nate's tone as by what he had said. "Why?" she asked.

"Don't tell me you haven't noticed half the men in this room can't keep their eyes off you!"

"That isn't my fault. I can't help it if—" She stopped, the most shattering thought coming to her. Was Nate... jealous?

"You hook men without even trying, don't you?" he said, the contempt in his voice mocking her stupid thoughts of his being jealous, dashing her hopes that she affected him in any other way than to arouse his dislike for what she had done to his brother.

"Well, at least we know there's no danger of your ever being caught on my hook, don't we?" she said tartly, swallowing her hurt.

JESSICA STEELE
is also the author of these

Harlequin Romances

Many of these titles are available at your local bookseller.

For a free catalogue listing all available Harlequin Romances
and Harlequin Presents, send your name and address to:

HARLEQUIN READER SERVICE
1440 South Priest Drive, Tempe, AZ 85281
Canadian address: Stratford, Ontario N5A 6W2

JESSICA STEELE

the other brother

Harlequin Books

TORONTO • LONDON • LOS ANGELES • AMSTERDAM
SYDNEY • HAMBURG • PARIS • STOCKHOLM • ATHENS • TOKYO

Harlequin Presents first edition September 1982
ISBN 0-373-10533-9

Original hardcover edition published in 1981
by Mills & Boon Limited

CHAPTER ONE

'YOU'RE just not with me, Kathryn.'

Hurriedly Kathryn straightened the small smile that hovered on her prettily shaped mouth. 'Sorry, Mr Kingersby,' she offered, while trying to recall what it was they had been doing before her thoughts had taken off to dream of what was to happen a week tomorrow.

'I wonder what it is you find far more thought absorbing than the celebrations of fifty years of Kingersby International we were discussing?'

Quickly she brought her mind back to the Jubilee to be celebrated in a couple of months' time—then saw the twinkle in his faded blue eyes and recognised that she was in for some more of his teasing. She saw from the way he was trying to repress a smile that he wasn't really cross with her for not paying attention. And because she was so happy anyway, she just had to let her own smile break; her smile was answer enough. He had been pulling her leg now in a nice way all week. She guessed next week would be no different.

'It couldn't be anything to do with the fact that that rascally nephew of mine has charmed his way into the heart of the prettiest secretary I've ever had, could it?' he went on.

'Er—it could be,' she tried to say demurely. But such was her happiness, she couldn't keep her smile from turning into a grin.

George Kingersby grinned too, his lined face creasing into more lines in his seventy-year-old face. Then, teasing apart, he asked, 'Did you say Rex is out of town?'

Kathryn nodded. 'Trying to finalise the Whitaker contract.'

'Thought that was already settled,' said the near to retiring chairman of Kingersbys, and her smile faded as she suspected censure for her fiancé.

'I'm sure it will be by this afternoon,' she said quietly.

'So am I,' he said confidently, and her smile started to peep out again that he hadn't been having a dig at Rex, realising that her sensitivities must be touchy where Rex was concerned. 'So what do you plan to do this weekend?' he asked, changing the subject.

'A million and one things,' Kathryn replied, wondering how she was going to get everything fitted in. If this was supposed to be a serene time for the bride then nobody had heard of the rushing around that accompanied having a big wedding.

'Name two,' said George, looking ready to offer his assistance, though from Kathryn's point of view everything that had to be done required her personal attention.

'Church rehearsal tomorrow,' she obliged. 'Plus another visit to the caterer's.'

With her mother dead, her father as far as she was concerned no longer anything to do with her, Kathryn felt it a matter of personal pride that she keep up her side of things on entering the very close knit Kingersby family, and pay for everything that was the responsibility of the bride's family herself. Rex had offered to pay for it all, of course; he could have done so without feeling the pinch. But she still had a little money from the amount her mother had left her and her sister Sandra. It would clear her out, but it was important to her that she settled her own dues. After she was married to Rex it would be a different matter... A smile curved her mouth again at just the thought of being married to Rex.

'You've gone from me again.'

'Er——' Hastily she came back. She recalled that Mr Kingersby had enquired what she had planned for the weekend, and added another couple of things she had to do to what she had already told him, 'And I must find time to go to see my sister in Reading. I collected the bridesmaids' dresses yesterday. This weekend will be the last chance I'll get to see if they fit my two nieces properly. And somehow,' she added, more pondering her thoughts out loud than thinking her employer would be interested, for all he was listening with every appearance of attention, 'I must try and take some of my things over to Rex's place. It will save me a lot of time next week if I do.'

'Stop!' said George, grinning again. 'You'll have me dizzy.' Then seriously, 'By the sound of it you're going to meet yourself coming back if you're not careful.' He thought for a moment, then told her, 'We've worked hard this week getting everything straight for the board meeting on Monday.' His face was suddenly puckish. 'What would you say if I offered you the rest of the day off?'

'Do you mean it?' She wasn't sure he wasn't still teasing her.

'Can you make use of the time?'

'Can I!'

'What's the use of marrying into the Kingersby empire if you can't have a few perks?'

Kathryn was so pleased she could have kissed him. 'I told Rex I might find time to pop a few things over to his flat tonight. He let me have a spare key before he went,' she beamed. 'I've got most of the things I shan't need ready packed, so I could take them over now and from there go on to Reading . . .' Her mind spun on.

'What are you waiting for?' said her lovely employer.

Staying only long enough to clear up her desk, check that there wasn't anything that could possibly be wanted before she came in again on Monday, by twelve-thirty Kathryn was driving her once-seen-better-days Mini out of the staff car park and heading homewards.

It was quiet in her flat, all other tenants in the building being still at work, but she quite liked the peace and quiet of it. Her rent was paid to the end of the month, a few weeks to go yet. But by the time her tenancy expired she would be in the sunny climes of Spain. Just she and Rex, together.

Thinking to have a bit of something when she got to Sandra's, Kathryn didn't bother with lunch, but got busy. Three trips down to her car with suitcases and cartons and she was wondering how on earth she had collected so much stuff, beginning to be thankful Rex's flat was so roomy. Finished at last, she checked to see she had the key Rex had given her, then she was off on the first leg of her journey.

Held up at some road workings, she let her mind wander freely in the interminable time it took for the temporary traffic lights to change.

Thoughts of George Kingersby's teasing made her smile. He hadn't done such a bad job with the firm he and his two brothers had started when they were young men fifty years ago, she mused. The other two, Rex's father one of them, were dead now. Her mind drifted on to the board meeting on Monday. Which one of the six cousins would get the chairmanship? she wondered. Rex had said he hadn't an earthly. Not that he wanted it. He was happier without that sort of responsibility, he had told her, and since there was nothing secret between them, had let her know that when it came the time to vote, he would be backing his brother Nate.

Would Nate get the chairmanship? she wondered. Or, as she had grown to think since listening to George singing his son's praises, would Adrian get it?

She was still toying with the answer as the lights changed allowing her to go forward. Would Nate want the job, always supposing Adrian hadn't already got it sewn up? Nate was seven years older than Rex—that made him thirty-seven. And if the streamlined way he ran the American end of the import and export business, not to mention the packaging business he had recently acquired for Kingersbys, was anything to go by, he could probably handle the chairman's job without any trouble. . . . Though her money was still on George's son Adrian.

Her mind flitted back to Rex's brother, a man she had never met. Nate was killing two birds with one stone by coming over for the meeting on Monday, she thought, and thoughts of her wedding never far from her mind taking over again, Nate was to be Rex's best man.

A pity she'd missed meeting Nate when he'd been over three months ago. It had all been arranged, Rex so proud and looking forward to introducing her to his brother. But it hadn't come off. Only an hour before she was due to meet him she had received a frantic phone call from Sandra saying her rake of a husband had walked out on her again. And as Sandra was unable to cope with the situation by herself her need of her had had to come first.

Kathryn's lips tightened when she thought of Victor Smith, her sister's husband. He was everything she disliked in a man. You'd have thought, she frowned, anger darting inside, that Sandra would have had more sense. Hadn't their father and the way he was constantly unfaithful to their mother been enough to show her if she couldn't have a constant husband then she was better off without marriage?

Broadminded about most things as she was, just the word infidelity was enough to have Kathryn feeling nauseous. Thank God she had found Rex. He would always keep faith with her, she knew it. Just as she knew that if there had been any doubt in her mind, even loving him as she did she would have turned him down. It was true, of course, that he had played around before they had met, he had told her as much. But there had been no one for either of them since they had become engaged. And Rex had known without her having even to mention it that no way was she going to have a marriage like that of her parents—or that of her sister.

As she reached the smart apartment block where Rex had his flat, the flat that after next Saturday she would set about making a home for them both, her smile peeped out again. And all the infidelity of her father, the unfaithfulness of her sister's husband—who had had his fling and then come home again; and to her amazement been taken back yet again by Sandra—went as she took a couple of suitcases from the boot and sent up glad thanks that the building had a lift so she wouldn't have to struggle three times up the stairs with her cargo.

Outside Rex's door she relieved herself of the weight she was carrying while she took out the door key from her bag. She smiled softly as she mused on the thought that Rex would be surprised to see her things when he came home tomorrow.

Though perhaps he wouldn't have a minute to spare to look into the spare room to see if she had found time to call and leave her things, she thought. And a sudden imp of mischief had her deciding to hang some item of hers beside his in his wardrobe.

Picturing his astonishment before his face creased into a smile as he went to change before meeting her at the church, to find one of her dresses hanging there, Kathryn unlocked the front door and went in.

Her eyes went straight to the door she knew to be his bedroom, a room he had showed her and had tried without success to get her to linger in, and she was still inwardly smiling at the surprise she was about to play on him as she closed the front door behind her. Her thoughts happy, not a cloud in her sky, she placed one case on the floor and headed for the bedroom with the other.

It was without conscious thought that she turned the door handle and pushed it inwards. She had actually taken three or four swinging steps inside the room before her eyes were drawn by a movement on the bed. And then she stared, and stared—horror-struck.

Disbelief was still inside her as she stood staring, knowing her eyes couldn't be lying. But even then she couldn't take in what her eyes were telling her. The scene she had walked in on was just refusing to register.

For long seconds her stunned brain refused to think—the couple sharing the bed appearing to be similarly dumb-struck. For the man she hadn't expected to see until they were in church rehearsing their responses tomorrow just sat and stared too, his chest bare while his blonde com-panion—his secretary, Kathryn recognised—tried to cover up her naked breasts.

Then as Kathryn went first ashen, then fiery red, and back to ashen again, Rex moved. And that was her cue to turn abruptly about.

He was in the sitting room with her before she could pick up her other suitcase and go back the way she had come through the flat door, a robe thrown about him as he grabbed hold of her arm.

'Kathryn,' he said hoarsely, dragging her round to face him.

And it was then that the most dreadful ice cold feeling took possession of her. She should be ranting and raving, she thought, even while this other person inside her looked icily down at that hand clutching on to her arm. So icy was her glance that as he saw her expression, Rex's grip on her loosened and his hand fell away.

'It would appear,' said the iceberg who had taken charge of her, 'that I'm the wrong person to be wearing this.' The automaton she had become took the ring from her engage-ment finger and handed it to him.

'*No!*' said Rex, a cry from the heart she was impervious to.

'Your next line, I believe, is, "Don't do this—I can explain". Or,' Kathryn said coldly, 'perhaps it's what you wanted. In my view you certainly aren't ready for marriage and the fidelity that word signifies.'

'Oh, for God's sake, Kathryn, don't be like this. Maxine means nothing to me . . .'

'Thanks very much,' said the blonde, who now appeared dressed in a bedcover at the doorway. And as two pairs of eyes turned to her she strolled into the room. 'You weren't saying that half an hour ago, nor were we just holding hands then—nor the many times before.'

'Oh, shut up!' Rex told her distractedly, turning from her, his eyes going imploringly to Kathryn. 'Don't—don't do this, Kathryn, please,' he begged. 'I love you. I . . . You love me.'

'Did I?' Kathryn answered, and thought that just about said it all as, her heart encased in a block of ice, she took the key he had given her and placed it on a low table to the side of her.

'Please, Kathryn . . .' Rex was still pleading when she picked up her other case and walked out.

Half an hour later she pulled her Mini to the side of the road. She had no idea where she was, had no recollection of driving or of even thinking. She was only aware of a feeling of being frozen up inside.

There were not even tears there at the dreadful shock she had received only a week before her wedding. Even the memory of how she had been congratulating herself that she had found one man she could utterly rely on to always be faithful didn't bring tears at the bitter knowledge of how badly she had been deceiving herself.

How long she sat there she couldn't have said. But at last, having to make a very conscious effort to stir herself, she just had to start to think.

She had been going to go somewhere after she had deposited her things, hadn't she? Where was she going? A need suddenly to see her sister reminded her that she had been going to go to Reading. But only then did she begin to understand fully why Sandra always rang her when she was in trouble. It was as though they both knew that whatever happened to them, the hurt and deception they endured, one thing was certain, each could rely on the other never to let them down.

Kathryn set the car in motion, found a signpost after about half a mile and then, able to sort out her directions, she turned her Mini and headed for Reading.

The ice that had formed inside had in no way diminished by the time she pulled on to the drive of her sister's home. And Sandra, hearing her car and coming to the door, her face showing pleased surprise at her unexpected arrival came smilingly forward, her eyes taking in the laden car.

'Goodness, Kathryn, how long are you stay . . .' She broke off as she saw Kathryn was having a hard time summoning up a smile for her. 'What's wrong?' she asked quickly. 'Something's happened, hasn't it?'

'You could say that,' Kathryn replied, getting out from the car. 'I've just come from finding my fiancé in bed with his secretary.'

'Oh—Kathryn!' Sandra's shocked disbelief was obvious. But, unable to handle her own emotional crises, she found the strength from somewhere to put her shock behind her for the moment. 'Come on, love,' she said gently, 'let's go inside. You can tell me about it over a cup of tea. We won't be disturbed, the girls are at a birthday party next door.'

Flatly, dry-eyed, Kathryn stirred the tea she didn't want and relayed without a flicker of emotion everything that had happened. As she came to the end she found that of the two of them it was Sandra who looked to be the one nearer to tears.

'Oh, love,' she crooned, looking lost for a way to comfort her. 'The wedding's off now, of course?' Her sister's look was sufficient answer, and both girls were silent for a while until Sandra enquired tentatively, 'Do you still love him?'

'I don't know what I feel,' Kathryn said tonelessly, 'Other than dead inside. I have an idea I should be tearing my hair out or something. But there's nothing there—I can't even cry.'

'You've had one almighty shock,' Sandra soothed. 'The tears will come, chick, don't rush them.'

Kathryn did her best to smile, knowing Sandra was upset on her behalf, but she would have welcomed tears as a relief from this nothing inside her. Then she found she was wondering what it would take to make her cry—there couldn't be a bigger disaster waiting round the corner for her, could there? Was she saving her tears for that?

She smiled mirthlessly at her thoughts, then went upstairs with Sandra to help get a room ready since she wouldn't hear of her going back to London that night.

Shortly after they had come down stairs, eight-year-old Marigold and six-year-old Gillie came bursting in. 'I recognised your car on the drive,' Marigold said in a rush, nearly falling over her words, the party she had been to promptly forgotten as she kissed her aunt and wanted to know if she had brought her bridesmaid dress with her.

'Of course I have,' Kathryn told her, forcing a bright smile. 'Though ... though ...' She floundered, not knowing how one broke the news to a young child that the wedding she had been so looking forward to being a bridesmaid at was now not going to take place.

'Aunty Kathryn and Uncle Rex have fallen out,' Sandra sped in to assist. 'They've decided not to get married after all.'

'Oh, bloomin' heck,' said Marigold, her disappointment echoed by shy little Gillie.

'But you can still have your dresses,' Kathryn put in quickly, seeing Gillie's face starting to crumple—and was glad, for all Sandra spoilt them dreadfully, that she instinctively understood she never wanted to see the dresses again and was quite firm with her daughters when she told them they could try the dresses on some other time.

Sandra tried when the girls had been put to bed to turn Kathryn's mind on to practical channels, telling her if she didn't want to be stuck with a massive bill from the caterers then she ought to get down to thinking about cancelling them without delay.

As she promised to write to them in the morning, the money she stood to lose was neither here nor there in her present frame of mind, Kathryn began to realise then that she had a whole lot of cancelling to think about. All she had cancelled so far was her engagement, and she hadn't had to think about that—it had been automatic.

In bed that night she tried to think along the practical lines Sandra had suggested. There were friends invited to the wedding to contact, presents to be returned. But try as she might to keep her mind on such matters, again and again the vision that had met her eyes that afternoon came back to haunt her.

How could Rex have deceived her so? How could he have taken Maxine Vernon to his bed?—Not just that one time either, if Maxine was to be believed, and with the evidence she had she saw no reason not to believe her. Though as far as she was concerned, once was more than enough.

To think, she thought dully, she had loved such a man— had loved him so that it had only been her strong sense of everything needing to be so right that had prevented her from sharing that same bed with him before the ceremony. Emotion seared her for the first time at the thought that she might well have committed herself to him only to find out too late that he wasn't to be trusted. Oh how glad she was she hadn't given in. If Rex couldn't wait those few months until the day they exchanged their vows, then he just wasn't the husband she had set her heart on having.

By the time she got up the next morning, the deep shadows under her eyes showed the terrible night she had spent. Victor Smith, her brother-in-law had been whisked briefly into the kitchen last night by Sandra and acquainted with the details and had then disappeared to his local. Though since there was no love lost between him and Kathryn, she on one occasion having the need to put him right when his wandering eye had wandered in her direction, she expected and got little sympathy from him. He was in the sitting room, thirty-two and already running to seed, when she went down.

'Good morning,' she said, giving him a brief glance and suffering the way his eyes went over her. It was the first chance he had had to try and needle her, and she wasn't at all surprised at the remark:

'So he slipped your noose, did he?'

'The choice in breaking our engagement was mine,' she said coldly, turning ready to go looking for Sandra.

'Had you let the poor bloke have what he wanted from you there'd have been no need for him to take his secretary between the sheets,' he jibed before she could escape, her hand already on the door handle. 'You're a hard-hearted bitch, Kathryn,' he sneered, determined to get a rise out of her.

She let her hand fall and turned to face him. She had never been afraid of him, and if there was any truth in what he said about Rex taking his secretary to bed in compensation for her, then Rex still wasn't the man she wanted to marry. But as for her being hard-hearted, she just couldn't believe that was true.

'No, you're wrong there,' she said, giving him a disdainful look so he would know he could count himself included. 'I'm not hard-hearted—just very particular.'

'But not so particular it stopped you from coming running for shelter under my roof,' Victor retorted, stung by her disdain. 'You know where to come when you need a shoulder to cry on.'

Where else should she go but to her sister? she wondered, trying to keep her temper since he had so rudely reminded her she was a guest in his house.

'Since Sandra has cried on my shoulder a good many times over you, I consider that's only fair, don't you?'

She didn't wait for any answer he had to that, but went in search of Sandra. She found her in the kitchen and felt a spasm of loving for her that after one look at her face her sister bit back the question she had clearly been going to ask on how had she slept, and instead explained, without knowing it, the reason for the acid she had just received from her husband.

'Vic's taking the girls into town this morning. I thought it would give you a chance to do any telephoning you might want to do in private.'

'There's no need for them to disappear on my account,' Kathryn said quickly, pangs of guilt smiting her that her visit was upsetting the whole household.

'He'll enjoy taking them out,' Sandra remarked from behind her rose-coloured lenses, not seeing as Kathryn did that Vic had probably planned to fry other fish that morning.

They didn't get a chance to discuss anything from then on as Gillie came in wanting help with her shoes. But it was quiet in the little detached house when they had waved them down the drive, and it was Sandra's practicality in problems that weren't directly her own that had her urging Kathryn to get started on what had to be done.

'People have got to be told before next Saturday,' she began. 'It'll be just too awful if . . .' Her sensitivity wouldn't let her finish.

'If they turned up at the church to find no bride or groom,' Kathryn made herself finish it for her. And though she jibbed at calling any of her friends on the telephone she was soon at work with the aid of Sandra's writing paper, finding that after the first three letters her task, though no more agreeable, became easier.

'What about Rex's family?' Sandra asked, seeing that all the envelopes so far were addressed to Kathryn's own friends and one aunt and uncle they rarely saw, but who had accepted an invitation. 'Aren't they coming from all over?'

'His brother Nate is coming from America with his cousin Adrian,' Kathryn said without much interest. 'And there's another cousin, Paul, who manages the French side of things. But none of them will have a wasted journey,' She broke off to explain briefly about the board meeting that was to be held on Monday to select a new chairman, glad to have a break from her letter writing. 'Rex,' she said, still feeling too iced up inside to feel any pain on saying his name, 'thinks Nate stands a chance of getting it, but with him making such a success of the American end, I can't see him wanting to give that up. And anyway, since Adrian is George's son I think it's more likely to go to him. Whatever happens they'll keep it in the family.'

'They're that close?'

'And how! When I first went to work there six months ago some optimistic company tried their hand at a take-over—talk about closing of ranks—they didn't stand a chance!' And going back to the cancelled wedding that wouldn't stray far from her mind, 'I'll let Rex tell his family. They'll all be there at the meeting on Monday anyway.' An unaccustomed cynicism entered her heart. 'It can come under the heading of "any other business".'

'Oh, love, don't be bitter,' Sandra cried. 'I know you've got cause, but don't let what's happened spoil you. Apart from this particular bee in your bonnet about fidelity you've always been more than generous about other people's short-comings.'

Not wanting to see Sandra upset, Kathryn squeezed her sister's hand, forcing a smile as she promised, 'I won't.' And she was about to get down to some more letter writing when from the look on Sandra's face something had just occurred to her.

'You say the Kingersbys are very close,' she brought out slowly.

'They don't call them the Magnificent Seven for nothing,' Kathryn agreed. 'I told you how no outsider would stand a chance once they gang together. Offend one and you offend them all . . .'

'Oh, love, what about your job?'

'My job?' For a second or two Kathryn didn't get her meaning. She hadn't yet got around to thinking about work. But following her sister's trend . . . 'I see what you mean,' she said thoughtfully.

'They won't sack you, will they?' And quickly, 'Oh, they wouldn't do that, would they? You've worked so hard and must be exceptionally good at your work to have got to be the chairman's secretary at only twenty-four. It would be wicked to sack you when it wasn't your fault.'

Kathryn's pensive brown eyes showed she didn't know whether breaking her engagement to the Marketing Manager of Kingersby International constituted grounds for them dismissing her or not—or even if she still wanted to work for them. The way she felt now she could bump into Rex in the building and walk straight by him without feeling a thing. But would that last?

She had at George Kingersby's request decided to stay on at the office after her marriage. She could remember now the thrill she had felt at the way he had said, 'Don't desert the office, Kathryn. It's about time we had a female Kingersby on the inside', but with the Kingersby blood affronted that she had broken off her engagement, would George still want her to stay with the firm?

'I don't know if they'll sack me or not,' she answered Sandra's question belatedly. 'To tell you the truth, I'm not sure I want to work there any more anyway.' The ice in her started to chip as her hands left her short dark hair to make a distracted movement. 'I'm just—not sure of anything any more.'

'What you need is a drink,' said Sandra bracingly. 'Shall we be a couple of devils and have a go at the cooking sherry?'

'Why not?' she answered, and getting on top of her moment of weakness, 'And after that I really will have the courage to ring my landlady and beg her to renew my tenancy.'

Saturday eventually passed. So too did Sunday. But when Kathryn began to make noises about going back to London she found that Sandra wouldn't hear of her going back to her empty flat that night. And chiefly because she had a suspicion that once back in her own surroundings then she would crack up, she was glad to fall in with her sister's urging that she stay another night.

It was as she was leaving the next morning, Sandra still in her dressing gown because it was so early having come out on to the drive to see her off, that Sandra revealed:

'I had thought Rex might at least have telephoned to see if you were with us this weekend.'

'It wouldn't have done him any good,' Kathryn said quietly, having hugged her and thanked her for being such a help that weekend, and putting her car into gear. 'As far as I'm concerned, Rex Kingersby has ceased to exist.'

CHAPTER TWO

KATHRYN let herself into the flat she had left so joyously on Friday. She looked around the sitting room, devoid now of those little touches that had made it home, and thought that presently she would go down to her car and collect the cardboard box of ornaments and knick-knacks that had gone to make that particular room look lived-in.

It was a blessing, she thought as she wandered despondently into the kitchen to make herself a cup of coffee, that her landlady had been taking her time selecting the next tenant. For Mrs Evans had said over the phone that she hadn't received all the references she had written for in respect of the future tenant and had not as yet re-let her flat.

So she still had a roof over her head, she mused, recalling though Mrs Evans had grumbled on a bit at the trouble she had put her to, she had agreed to let her rescind her notice.

She tried to think if there was anything else she had to do in cancelling the arrangements, but between them she and Sandra seemed to have thought of everything. Dear Sandra, she'd been a pillar of strength this weekend.

Still trying to think practically the way her sister had steered her, Kathryn recalled how she had decided on the drive from Reading that she just couldn't go into the office today. Facing all those Kingersbys was beyond her. But the professionalism with which she tackled her work demanded that she at least ring through to George Kingersby and tell him she wouldn't be in.

The kettle boiled, but she turned it off, not sure she wanted to sit over a solitary cup of coffee that would give her too much time to think, and went instead to sit near her phone in the sitting room, her mind busy while waiting for business to start that day in considering what she was going to say to George.

Nine o'clock arrived, and with it came a feeling of sickness as she wondered what story Rex had concocted, a certainty grown in her that he would not have given his uncle the true reason for her handing him back his ring. All the Kingersbys were proud, and Rex was no exception. He wouldn't, she knew then with a definite sureness, want any one of them knowing what he had been up to.

With nausea welling up inside at the thought that she might be called on to give her side of it, Kathryn knew two things as she quelled the feeling of wanting to be sick. One was that none of the Kingersby clan would believe her, and two, that her own personal pride would never have her breathing a word of that sordid scene to anyone outside her own family.

She dialled the Kingersby International number, half of her of the opinion that George had already delegated some-one else to take notes at the board meeting scheduled for eleven o'clock.

'Mr George Kingersby, please—Kathryn Randle,' she told the answering switchboard operator, and tilted her chin in case the first words she heard from her boss were that she could come and clear out her desk.

'Kathryn! Kathryn, where are you?'

There was none of the hostility she had half been ready for in George Kingersby's voice. But she held on to her pride, fairly certain that there would be before this call was finished. For if he didn't know yet that there wasn't to be any wedding on Saturday, then as she saw it, she was going to have to be the one to inform him of that fact.

'I'm at my flat,' she answered. 'I've just returned after spending the weekend . . .'

'Well thank God you're back,' he cut in and went on, to her surprise, 'We've been trying to contact you since Friday evening, but apart from your saying something about going to Reading, you could have been in Timbuktu for all the success we've had.'

'You've been trying to contact me?' Surely the Kingersbys weren't ganging up to try and make her change her mind!

'My dear . . .' Suddenly George's voice had taken on a gentle note. 'Have you heard yet about Rex?'

'Rex?' A premonition of some sort of disaster prickled along her spine. Pride departed as in a low whisper she managed, 'I haven't seen Rex since Friday. We . . .'

'I know that. Haven't we been in touch with everyone you said you were going to see, left messages all over the place . . .' He broke off as though thinking this was getting them nowhere. 'Kathryn, my dear, I'm sorry to be the one to have to tell you—but Rex has had a very serious motor accident.'

For a moment she was robbed of speech. Shocked by what she had heard, she was shaken too that even hearing such news had not managed to fracture the ice that encased her heart. Oh, she felt sorrow that he had been hurt, but shatteringly it didn't go deeper than it would have done had she heard the same news about any one of a dozen of her acquaintances.

'Are you still there, Kathryn?'

'Yes—yes, I'm still here.'

'I know this must be a dreadful shock for you, but . . .'

'How badly is he hurt?' she asked quickly, and as a dreadful thought struck, for although she felt nothing for him at that moment she didn't want that he should be . . . 'He's not—dead, is he?'

'No, no,' she was assured. And George went on to tell her that Rex had somehow managed to turn his car over, no

other car being involved, which left them to think he had
swerved to avoid some bird or animal in the road. The end
result was that he had multiple injuries, that it had been
touch and go over the weekend and that in the few occasional
moments of consciousness, he had been calling for her.

'H-have you heard how he is this morning?' Kathryn
asked, guilt she hadn't earned swamping her that he might
still be at death's door and she hadn't been around to give
him that last-minute comfort.

'I rang the hospital before I left home,' George told her,
mentioning the name of the hospital where Rex had been
taken. 'They tell me that at last he's beginning to show signs
of life. It's going to be a long job, Kathryn, but I'm sure
he's going to be all right.'

She heard the sympathy in his voice for her, and knew it
as a wasted emotion on her behalf. But she just could not
now, in the light of what he had just told her, explain to him
that she was no longer engaged to his nephew.

'Would you mind if I don't come into work today?' she
asked.

'Of course not, my dear. I wouldn't expect you to. You'll
be wanting to get round to the hospital as soon as I've put
this phone down.'

Perhaps it was as well George Kingersby didn't stay
talking after that. For as she put down her phone, Kathryn
knew the greatest reluctance to go anywhere near the
hospital.

Sandra's husband had called her a hard-hearted bitch.
But she knew she wasn't. She was not hard-hearted enough,
if the truth was known. And that was the reason she didn't
want to go anywhere near that hospital. For she knew, even
frozen up inside as she felt about Rex, that if she went to the
hospital, saw his broken body, his needing her, from what
George had said, then she could very clearly see that she
would be in danger of forgetting her own feelings and

would be wearing his ring again for no matter how many weary long months it took him to recover. Months when that other side of her would loathe, detest every moment that ring was on her finger.

Guilt attacked again as she fought against the weakness of going to his side to give what comfort she could. But the scene in his flat, Maxine Vernon in bed beside him, so obviously without a stitch on, had guilt being chased away, had her hunting up the hospital's phone number before guilt could attack again.

She was through to the private ward, speaking with the Sister-in-charge before she got round to wondering if they would tell her anything anyway or just fob her off with 'As well as can be expected.'

But she had reckoned without her name being so much spoken of that weekend that everyone attending Rex knew that if Miss Kathryn Randle appeared she was to be shown into his room without delay.

So on telling the efficient-sounding Sister her name, explaining that she had only just heard from Mr George Kingersby of the accident, she discovered the Sister was prepared to tell her everything to put her mind at rest.

'I think we can safely say he's out of the wood now,' Sister said optimistically. 'Of course it will take a long time for his broken bones to mend and for us to have him walking again. But his condition is no longer critical.'

Relief swooped in as Kathryn realised Rex was going to recover without the need for her to go to him, to perjure the honesty in her soul by pretending she still wanted to be engaged to him.

'He's—he's not likely to have a relapse, is he?' A softness in her she didn't want forced the question.

'I shouldn't think so for a moment,' she was informed briskly, as if that was something Sister just would not allow. 'Not now he's turned the danger corner. He's fully conscious and has the greatest will to live of any man his age that I've seen.'

'Thank you, Sister,' Kathryn said quietly, and put down the phone.

So that was that. Rex would get better without her help. Nothing was unchanged save that instead of Rex telling his family the wedding was off, it very much looked as though she was going to have to do it.

Not that he was in any position to put in an appearance at the church next Saturday anyway. But the straight and uncomplicated way she ran her life wouldn't put up with the Kingersbys not knowing. And for all she couldn't see her telling George just why she had broken her engagement—stood a very big risk of losing her job that she'd dared to throw a Kingersby over—she knew that tomorrow she would be telling George, and through him the rest of the family, she had dared to do exactly that.

Feeling in the need of that cup of coffee, she got up to go to re-heat the kettle. But barely had she set her coffee cup down on the small table in her sitting room when a hard no-nonsense banging on the door of her flat thundered through the panelling.

For a moment she stood rooted, the sound was so un-expected with most of the other tenants at work. Not that any of her fellow flat dwellers ever banged on her door like that anyway. Somebody must have left the front door open, she realised, something that often happened, other-wise whoever was out there selling something would have had to ring the outside doorbell.

But when she opened the door to the tall, good-looking man who stood there, something in his features familiar, though not in the ice-cold blue eyes that roved over her and took her apart without bothering to put her back together again, she knew at once this was no door-to-door salesman.

'Are you Kathryn Randle?' he questioned abruptly, and ignited an instant anger in her by the way he looked at her as if he had seen much better things swimming about in a stagnant pool, as by the sheer unadulterated aggression emanating from him.

'And what if I am?' she challenged, trying to remember where she had met him before while wondering how it was possible she had ever forgotten meeting such a mentally and physically alive-looking person.

'If you are Kathryn Randle you can start by telling me where the hell you've been this weekend.'

She had it then. She never had met him before—but he was a Kingersby, that was for sure. They all looked like each other. Though this one had got far more aggression, far more an air of knowing what he wanted, of going after it and getting it, than any of them. And she knew in that moment of recognising him as one of the "gang together" Kingersby men that one would have to stand one's ground with this one or run the risk of being trampled on.

'What's it to do with you where I've been?' she asked sharply, having no intention of letting him into her flat with his mammoth aggression looking for an outlet.

'Every damn thing,' he told her roughly. 'Had you been in any of the places you were supposed to be, my brother would have been very much less stressed than he was.'

So this was Nate! And because he was Rex's closest living relative she had been looking forward to meeting—him!

'You'd better come in,' she said. And she began at that moment to dislike Nate Kingersby so much as he closed the door once he was inside, that when she was fully determined not to let him in there was something in him that had her doing the opposite from what she intended.

She turned when he was a few steps into the room, catching the way his eyes flicked round what must seem to

him to be a cold and cheerless place without so much a vase
or an ornament to brighten it up.

'Exactly where were you this weekend?' he demanded
more than asked, his hands thrust deep into his pockets
adding to the aggressive look of him. 'And don't give me
the cock and bull story you gave my uncle on Friday that
you were visiting your sister in Reading. The job you had
to do there wouldn't have taken until this morning.'

'Why should I tell you anything?' Never had Kathryn
known a man who could so instantly have her standing up to
him. 'It's obvious that whatever I tell you you're not going
to believe me.'

His eyes glinted at that. But she wasn't afraid of him. 'It
must have been something very important to have you
ignoring the arrangements that had been made for the
church rehearsal on Saturday,' he fired, and without waiting
for her to say anything, was demanding, 'What was it that
had you breaking that appointment?'

'If . . .' Kathryn found she was angry enough to tell him.
But she just didn't get the chance.

'You had to have your last-minute fling, didn't you?' Nate
Kingersby rapped. 'Or wasn't it last-minute?' His hands
came out of his pockets and she didn't like at all the way
they were so ominously clenched. But he took her mind
completely off them by shocking her with, 'Were you
hoping to keep your lover and a husband?'

'L-lover?' she spluttered, astounded, barely able to
credit that this vile man was accusing her of not being
around this weekend because she had been . . . 'How—how
dare you!' she started furiously, then found her outrage
ignored as he lost patience with what he must think of as
her act of innocence.

'Are you aware,' he said furiously, 'that while you were
having a high old time wherever it was you disappeared to,
your fiancé has met with a serious accident?'

The heat went out of her. She had known all along about
the closeness of the Kingersbys. Rex's pain would be
Nate's pain—pain he found release from by turning it into
anger against her. She was, he thought, the one who could
have eased his brother's suffering.

'Yes, I know,' she answered quietly. 'I telephoned the
hospital a short while ago.'

'You know? You telephoned . . .?' he exclaimed, taken
aback, and Kathryn saw in him then the dark clouds that
were gathering before the storm that was about to break
over her head. 'Then why in the name of thunder haven't
you visited him?' His voice was barely controlled as he
grated, 'What by all that's holy are you doing sitting here
drinking coffee?' His eyes had missed nothing, she saw.
'Why are you still here when you should be over at that
hospital by my brother's bedside?'

He was right, of course—from the view he had of their
engagement. And so strongly did the dominating force of
the man come across, she almost said she would go and
visit Rex. But her feeling of having been so terribly let
down by what she saw as Rex's betrayal of her, not counting
her views on fidelity inside and outside marriage, her
heartbroken mother, Sandra going the same way unless she
soon saw sense, had her finding sufficient will to hold out
against him.

'I won't be going to see him,' she said woodenly—and
had to harden her heart further when he looked at her
incredulously the moment before he barked:

'My God, what has my brother got himself engaged to?
Talk about being blinded by love . . .' And then it seemed
he had finished playing. 'Get your coat,' he commanded.
'I'm taking you to see him right now.'

Stubbornly Kathryn refused to move. 'I'm not going,'
she defied him, and only just managed not to flinch when
she saw his firm chin square meaningfully as he came a step

nearer, his hands looking as though any minute they would come up around her throat and begin to throttle her.

'Don't play games with me, Miss Randle,' he bit at her, 'I warn you now I'm in no mood for them. My brother has been going out of his mind calling for you these last two days. If you have any intention of becoming his wife—though God help him, for we're powerless to interfere if it's you he wants—then you'll find some small scrap of decency in you and come with me now.'

Kathryn knew then that she was fighting for her future peace of mind by sticking fast to her determination not to go with him. He was strong, was Nate Kingersby, forceful, with a will of iron. Give into him once and she might find she was forgiving Rex, and even though feeling nothing for him, marrying him. So even while his talk of Rex going out of his mind calling for her stirred her sympathy, she was heartily glad she had phoned the hospital and learned that his condition was improving. Nate's dig about her sense of decency didn't dent her.

Stonily she faced the man who looked ready to drag her by the hair to his brother's bedside. And she knew then that the information she had been going to impart to George Kingersby tomorrow was going to find its way to the family through another source. There was no other way Nate was going to leave her flat without her.

'I think I'd better tell you,' she said, emotion well out of her voice, 'that—that I no longer consider myself engaged to Rex.'

'You're . . .'

For a moment what she had said stopped him dead in his tracks. Then she saw the quick intelligence in that high forehead do some rapid mental arithmetic. But she nearly dropped when he brought out the sum total of his additions.

'I see,' he said, and his voice was coldly sneering as he brought out, 'So you've telephoned the hospital, learned only half the information, and from what you've heard have decided for yourself just how bad things are with my brother.'

'They said . . .' she began, nowhere near to knowing what thoughts were going through his head.

'They've told you,' he cut in, 'about his broken bones, and from that you've decided he's going to be a cripple for life.'

'No!' Her reply was prompt. But she found Nate was either too angry with her, or just wasn't interested in any denials she had to make.

He took that stride nearer. It was all he needed to have him close enough to grab hold of her arms in a brutish hold.

'Are you afraid he'll be so crippled he won't be good in bed any more?' he jibed, his hands biting into her.

'In bed!' she gasped. And, astonished, 'Any more?' Her arms where he held her were hurting like crazy, but she was too staggered by what he was suggesting had gone on between her and Rex to think of doing anything about getting free.

'Between brothers little is sacred,' he went on, his lip curling as he looked down his straight arrogant nose as though wondering what any Kingersby should see in her that he should want to take her to bed. 'Rex told me the last time I was home that he was going short of—nothing.'

Kathryn felt her colour leave her, nausea striking as she wrenched out of his hold. She presented him with her back, nowhere near to coming to terms with the fact that Rex had been so ready to boast about his sexual prowess to his brother, it hadn't bothered him one tiny bit that he had given him the impression that as well as being betrothed, they were lovers.

'Would you please go,' she told Nate Kingersby over her shoulder.

And not trusting herself not to play the same character

blackening game as Rex. Afraid suddenly, pricked by his
careless boasting that she might forget herself and tell his
brother that the 'nothing' Rex was going short of was
being taken care of by his secretary, that Maxine Vernon
had been his bed partner, not her, Kathryn went quickly
across the room intending to shut herself in her bedroom
until he had gone.

The sight of her wedding dress hanging on the outside of
her wardrobe so as not to crush it pulled her up short as she
opened the door. And the tears she had known would have
to come soon started to her eyes, and the ice in her swiftly
melted.

'You'd have worn white too,' said a cynical voice by her
right shoulder, doing more than she ever could to stem her
tears.

'It doesn't matter now what I would have worn, does it?'
she said, fighting hard not to break down until he had gone.
'The wedding is off—permanently.'

'Rex isn't going to be a cripple,' that hateful sneering
voice came back rapidly.

'I know that,' she answered, and found pride had to be
heard. 'I gave him his ring back on Friday.'

She wished pride had stayed down when strong, savagely
hard masculine hands clamped down on her shoulders and
twisted her to face him.

'You bitch!' he snarled. 'So that's why he went out and
got so roaring drunk he smashed himself up.' His blue
eyes glinted white flame. 'Who the *hell* do you think you
are, that you can jilt a Kingersby a week before the
wedding.'

Having not so far been afraid of him, Kathryn knew real
fear then as those hands left her shoulders and closed round
her throat. She couldn't even manage a squeak, she was so
frightened. Wide terrified brown eyes stared into his, her
colour gone as those hands gripped. Then suddenly she was

free, pushed away to stagger backwards into her bedroom.

'You're not worth serving a prison sentence for,' Nate Kingersby reviled her. 'But just remember this, Miss Kathryn Randle—nobody, and I mean nobody, does the dirty on a Kingersby without living to regret it—ever. You're going to regret the day you ever jilted one of us— *believe it*.'

He had been gone all of ten seconds before she started to breathe anywhere near normally again. And then she turned—turned and saw once more her white wedding dress, a dress bought when her dreams had been many. And a dry sob left her, followed by another. And suddenly there was no ice. She was weeping as though her heart would break.

The rest of that day found Kathryn cleaning and polishing an already immaculate flat, making several trips to her car and returning her belongings to their usual places. But try to keep busy as she did, again and again her thoughts would return to that beast of a man, Nate Kingersby.

She'd handled it all wrong, she thought too late. Yet how else could she have handled it? He had looked angry enough to strangle the life out of her. And although it sounded ridiculous now his threatening presence wasn't around, she had an awful feeling had she told him the truth of her broken engagement, those fingers around her throat would have tightened to choke the life out of her at what he would have considered her attempt to blacken his brother's name.

No, she thought, putting the last of her clothes away, it was much better to let him go on his way thinking, as he must, that she had jilted his brother because she thought more of the man she was supposed to have shared her weekend with than she did of Rex.

But she felt more confused then, even when her thoughts centred on Rex, as they were bound to on and off throughout that day. On Friday she had been so in love with him—

or so she had thought. Yet here it was Monday and it wouldn't bother her if she never saw him again. Her tears, her heartbreak, she realised hours later, must have been on account of dashed dreams. Dashed dreams, plus coming out of the shock that had gripped her on seeing the man she had so wholeheartedly trusted in bed with his secretary. And while she couldn't help but feel sorry for him that he probably had months of lying in hospital to look forward to, she couldn't help that that sorrow was tinged with disgust that Rex could have allowed his brother to think she was his mistress as well as his fiancée.

She could see now too why he had told Nate what he had. But the tremendous respect she had had for Rex took another dip that having his share of the Kingersby pride, he had felt his masculinity impaired that he couldn't get her into his bed, had had to boast about his prowess knowing full well that Nate would think it was she who was withholding 'nothing'.

By the time Tuesday morning came around, after hours spent in soul-searching thought, Kathryn had come to one very certain conviction. She could never have loved Rex Kingersby so completely as she had thought. She had, after tearing herself apart in self-analysis, come to the conclusion that because he had appeared to have all the fine qualities she was looking for in her future mate, she had let herself believe it was love she felt for him.

She got out of bed knowing that now she had things clear in her mind, all ends were not nearly as neatly tied up as she would like them to be. She still had to go in to work, still had to face George Kingersby. There was no knowing what Nate had told him, but as she bathed, dressed and left her flat, the thought returned that she wouldn't be at all surprised to find she would shortly be back at her flat and out of a job.

Knowing she was too proud to sit at her desk and wait to

be called into George's office to receive her dismissal, Kathryn stopped by her desk only to compose herself. And still carrying her handbag, still in her topcoat against a sharp frosty April morning, she crossed the carpet, tapped briefly on his door, and went in.

'Good morning, Kathryn,' George greeted her mildly, and for all his face was serious as she answered his greeting, she felt some of her tension leaving that he was looking less severe than she had expected.

'D-did Nate tell you he called to see me yesterday?' came blurting from her, revealing that some of her tension was still around.

'He tells me you and Rex are no longer engaged,' he said by way of confirmation that Nate must have filled him in on everything.

She took a steadying breath. 'You'll be wanting my resignation?' The words left her quietly. Words that had to be said, as unflinchingly she brought out what she thought was a fact.

'Nate tells me you broke your engagement before Rex had his accident. Is that true?'

Kathryn blinked at the question. She was astounded that even without doubt believing what Nate had told him, here was one Kingersby who looked prepared to listen to any mitigating circumstances there might be.

Still unable to believe it, she asked, 'He told you I'd been away with—with some other man for the weekend?' And then felt a glow start inside that the old man she had worked for for only six months had seen something in her that had him questioning what he had been told by his own kin.

'Not you, Kathryn,' George told her, his face still serious. 'I'd stake my life on your integrity. And while I'll admit it grieves me that anyone should inflict pain on any one member of my family, I want to hear from your own lips exactly what went on to cause the eager young woman who left this office on Friday anticipating with joy in her heart her forthcoming wedding to suddenly change her mind.' There was a shrewdness in his face that told her nothing but the truth would do. 'It was you who broke the engagement and not the other way around, wasn't it?' he questioned severely.

'Yes,' she answered quietly.

'Why?'

The question was blunt. And looking at his faded blue eyes, eyes she noted for the first time that held a hurt pride that anyone could reject a member of that tightly integrated family, she just knew she couldn't tell him. Here, she saw, was someone who might believe her. But she couldn't do it. For suddenly George looked frail and old. Of course he must have spent a worried weekend wondering if Rex was going to pull through, and that probably accounted for the way he looked more tired and worn than she had ever seen him. But the Kingersbys prided themselves on their honour. To tell him the truth about the nephew he loved almost as much as he loved his own sons would wound him deeply, and she just couldn't do it.

'I'm sorry, Mr Kingersby,' she said softly, and, unable to lie to him either. 'It's something far too personal for me to want to talk about.'

For long moments after her unsatisfactory answer George Kingersby sat and stared at her sensitive face. Then, 'Very well,' he said at last, 'we'll leave it for the moment.' And, suddenly a business man again, 'In the meantime perhaps we should get on with some work.'

'You mean . . .' she gasped not quite taking it in. 'You mean I still have my job?'

For the first time in what had been a taut ten minutes, George smiled. 'There may have been times when I've been a bit of a Tartar, Kathryn, but I hope you'll never accuse

me of being unfair.' And while delight entered her being
that the instant dismissal she had been expecting was not to
be, he went on, 'And anyway, with the new chairman
taking over very shortly, I want everything ship-shape and
Bristol fashion when he comes in.'

'You had the meeting yesterday after all?' she asked,
realising at the same time that even with one member of the
board absent business had to go on.

About to congratulate him on his son Adrian getting the
job, certain in her own mind that would be the case, she
checked, an ominous apprehension taking her.

'Er—your son, Adrian,' she brought out slowly, yet
still ready with her congratulations, 'He *is* to be the new
chairman, isn't he?'

'As a matter of fact, no,' said George, looking in no way
put out that his eldest son hadn't been appointed. 'Adrian
will take over the American side of things.' And while her
feeling of apprehension grew, calmly, he dropped out, 'By
an entirely unanimous decision, my nephew Nate is to be
the new chairman.'

Kathryn went to her desk, only just keeping from letting
the retiring chairman see the horror she was feeling at the
bombshell he had dropped. Nate Kingersby was shortly to
be the new chairman. And she, her senses reeled, and she—
was she to be secretary to that brute of a man?

CHAPTER THREE

By the time lunchtime came around, familiar with her work and having coped with it semi-automatically, Kathryn took herself off for a walk. Her appetite gone, there was one very clear fact only staring her in the face: she was going to lose her job anyway.

Mr Kingersby's judgment of her had swayed in her favour against his loyalty to his family. He must have seen something in her that told him she wasn't the hard case Nate had made her out to be. He hadn't sacked her anyway. But she just knew she wouldn't fare so well with Nate. The minute he was in, she would be out.

At the end of her lunch hour she headed back to her office on the top floor, knowing there was only one way left open for her. She had her pride too. She wasn't waiting for Nate Kingersby to tell her to take a long walk on a short pier.

Mr Kingersby only ever had a sandwich for lunch, so she would go in now and tell him, she decided. She had about eight or nine weeks left, she calculated. George would want to stay on for the golden jubilee, would want to complete his fifty years in harness. But when he left, then so would she.

Entering her office, she paused only to drop her handbag down and hang up her coat. Then tapping briefly on the door as she had that morning, she went in.

Then what she had come in to say disappeared entirely from her mind—for she would recognise that tall lofty figure anywhere. That broad-shouldered man standing immaculate in his light grey suit, his back to her as he stared out of the window, wasn't George Kingersby.

Nate Kingersby turned, his eyes contemptuous as,

38

unspeaking, he looked her over before lifting his head a
fraction as though that was all he need do to enquire of such
a lightweight what she wanted.

'I was looking for Mr Kingersby,' she said, a flicker of
anger beginning to niggle inside at his insolent appraisal.

'You've found him,' he drawled, misunderstanding her
on purpose she knew.

'Mr George Kingersby,' she said tautly, wondering if he
would still manage to look as insolent if she took a swipe at
him as every instinct urged.

'He's out,' he told her, not trying to hide that he was
being deliberately difficult.

Putting her head in the air, Kathryn turned. He wasn't the
chairman yet, and until he was she had no intention of
suffering him more than she had to.

'What did you want him for?'

The question was aimed at her departing back. But with
her head still high Kathryn turned about, and with abou
as much sweetness as an overgrown stick of rhubarb told
him shortly:

'I wanted to tell him I'm resigning.'

'So you do have a small supply after all,' Nate came back,
so obviously impervious to her snappy answer that she
found she was gritting her teeth before she asked:

'What do you mean by that?'

'I had thought you totally lacking in decency,' he
enlightened her bluntly.

She stalked back to her desk and barely waited to be
seated before she was slamming into her typewriter. The
swine, went her furious thoughts as the keys hammered
down. The unmitigated swine! To insinuate that it was a
spark of decency she had dredged up from somewhere that
compelled her to give in her notice!

Her eyes sparking, she yanked the paper from her typewriter added her signature, then thrust it inside an envelope.

The next second she was leaving her seat and marching into the other office to place the envelope down where George Kingersby was bound to see it the moment he came in. She was nearly out through the door again when that insolent voice was heard once more.

'Just why was it you jilted my brother?'

Kathryn stopped in her tracks. She turned round, and soon saw that Nate Kingersby was no nearer to being ready to believe anything she told him today than he had been the day before.

'I thought you'd cleverly worked that out for yourself yesterday,' she said, refusing to be browbeaten when his eyes narrowed at her sarcastic tone. 'Didn't you decide yesterday that I threw him over because I'd had a better offer?'

The murderous look that came into his eyes told her he wasn't about to start being civil to her. But before he could begin to flatten her with one of his none too polite phrases, the outer door opened and George Kingersby came in.

Kathryn managed a smile for him as she passed on her way back to her desk. She heard him say, 'Sorry to keep you, Nate, you know how it is when one gets chatting.' The door closed, but it was a full five minutes before she had cooled down sufficiently to give her work the full concentration it deserved, and even then she was on edge waiting for that door to open.

When it did she wouldn't have been at all surprised if Nate Kingersby had stopped by her desk to fire a departing shot. But he didn't. She looked up when he approached her desk, saw he was looking straight at her, and felt a momentary discomfort before a surge of temper sapped it as he went out. For the first time in her life a man had looked straight through her as though she didn't exist.

Then her own feelings had to be put to one side, for George, her letter of resignation in his hands, had come out of his office too.

'What's this?' he asked without preamble, for all the message it contained was self-explanatory.

It was on the tip of her tongue to say there was no way she was going to work for Nate when he retired. But she was all too conscious that George Kingersby's loyalty to his family had been stretched more than enough by keeping her on after she had broken her engagement to his other nephew. To start implying that Nate was the swine she knew him to be would have her parting very bad friends with George, and she had grown too fond of him in the short time she had worked for him to want to part bad friends if that could be avoided.

'I—I think it's for the best, Mr Kingersby,' she told him quietly instead.

Sadly he shook his head. 'There's no need for you to leave. It'll be six months or more before Rex is back, if fear of meeting him again is what's worrying you.'

'It isn't that,' she started to deny, but she saw she wasn't being believed, and had to bite down hard not to tell him the real reason.

'Won't you stay on a little while longer?' he asked. 'I'll give you my word we won't try and hang on to you once Rex is up and about and likely to pay the office a visit.' And before she could find any convincing argument without revealing her true feelings about the new chairman, he was saying, 'I'll let you into a little secret, Kathryn—I'm taking the remainder of my time as chairman on some weeks spent on catching up on all the holidays I've missed over the years. Well, a few weeks, anyway,' he tacked on.

'You're going . . .'

'I've this week and next week to complete in my guise as chairman, then off to sunnier climes. I shall be back for the jubilee, though, wouldn't miss that for the world!'

Kathryn had to give him an answering smile. He deserved his holiday—goodness knew he had earned it. He should

have retired years ago, but he had loved his work so much he
had stayed on. But this was getting nothing settled about
her resignation.

'That means I only have a fortnight left to work for you,'
she said, trying to remember if she was legally bound to give
a month's notice or if she could get away with giving only
two weeks.

George nodded. 'That's why I feel it's important you
stay on,' he said. 'Nate has to return to the States to help
ease Adrian in and to clear up a few loose ends. So there's a
very good chance that I shall be away before I have time to
show him the way things run this end.' He was solemn all at
once as he added, 'I was rather banking on you, my dear,
to assist him in the change-over. You're good at the work—
"excellent" I don't think is stating the case too highly. I
should certainly enjoy my holiday more if I knew you were
on hand to help with anything Nate can't be expected to be
au fait with until he's been in the chair awhile.' And, his
voice taking on a coaxing note, 'Would you have my holiday
ruined worrying how Nate was coping without a secretary
who knows where everything is?'

So much for the hardhearted label her brother-in-law
would have hung around her neck, Kathryn thought, and
her heart-strings tugged as she looked as George's tired face
and saw that he looked more than ready for a strain-free
holiday.

'But—but I—don't think Nate likes me well enough to
have me working for him,' she said, holding back the truth,
that his dislike of her went treble as far as she was concerned.

George looked puzzled as he peered into her worried
brown eyes. Then with a fatherly gesture he patted her
hand. 'Did he give you a bad time yesterday?' And when her
eyes gave him the reply, he patted her hand again. 'Isn't
that understandable? Nate and Rex have always been close.
I don't think it would be exaggerating to say Nate had little

sleep over the weekend worrying if Rex was going to pull through. When he wasn't at his brother's bedside he was haring around looking for you—can you blame him that he gave you a bit of a tough time when he eventually caught up with you?'

Bit of a tough time! His uncle hadn't seen him with his hands around her throat! Nor had he been around an hour ago when Nate had insinuated that to give in her notice was the least she could do.

And she remembered, without difficulty, the way Nate had said, 'No one does the dirty on a Kingersby without living to regret it.' She knew then that if she stayed on she would be made to rue the day.

'I . . .' she began. But before she could add 'must leave', George was pulling at those heart-strings with a vengeance.

'If you're determined to go there's nothing I can do to stop you, my dear. Though it will mean, I'm afraid, I shall have to give very serious thought to cancelling the holiday both I and my wife were so looking forward to.'

Kathryn had met Dora Kingersby several times, a delicate-looking little lady who had probably had as few holidays as George in those early years.

'All right,' she said, those two words out before she had given herself time to think. It didn't enter her head then that her employer wasn't above being a shade wily to get his own way. 'I'll stay for . . .'

'For three months at least,' said George, suddenly beaming.

'For three months,' she found herself promising. If Nate Kingersby hadn't found his feet by then—hard luck!

Though as she made her way home that night, she was already beginning to regret her promise. If she was truthful, she had regretted it within five minutes of giving her word. But, she consoled herself, if everything she had heard about

Nate Kingersby's astute business brain was true, he wouldn't need her assistance very much anyway. And why was she worrying anyway? If that brief slanging match she'd had with him today was anything to go by, she wouldn't have to stick it out for three months—he would be giving her the order of the boot within the first five minutes of his taking charge.

The state of Rex's recovery had not been mentioned that day. And since the moment hadn't come up when she could ask without George perhaps thinking that for someone who had terminated a relationship she was showing an unexpected interest, after she had her meal Kathryn rang the hospital to enquire personally.

It wasn't that she had any particular interest in Rex, she thought, as she waited for her call to be put through, but that now her shocked senses were at last sorted out, she knew that while she no longer cared deeply about him, and disliked very much that he could boastfully have given his brother the impression he had, it just wasn't in her to hate the man she had once been engaged to.

'Physically Mr Kingersby is progressing satisfactorily,' the ward Sister told her in answer to her enquiry. 'But he has been a little depressed today,' she further informed her, then went on cheerfully, 'Though that isn't unusual at this stage. I'm sure he'll pick up tomorrow.'

Kathryn put down the phone, remembering the way Rex had never been down, and hoping sincerely that he would soon be over his depression.

Next she telephoned her sister and had a long chat with her, acquainting her with the news of Rex's accident. And hearing sympathy in Sandra's voice for any more heartbreak she might be suffering, she felt bound to confess that, unbelievable as it still seemed to her, she just did not feel that way about Rex any more.

'Well, I must say I'm relieved to hear it,' Sandra remarked, sounding as relieved as she'd said. 'Er—was there any trouble at work, by the way?'

'I still have a job, if that's what you mean,' Kathryn told her, and went on to relate most of what had happened that day. Though for some unknown reason she held back on the subject of what a brute Nate Kingersby was.

After her call to Sandra she wandered into her bedroom. She might as well have an early night. Heaven knew she had hours of missed sleep over the weekend and last night to catch up on. By the sound of it George would have her working flat out until he left, a week on Friday. And she groaned aloud at the weakness in her that had her promising to work for Nate Kingersby for *three whole months*!

She cheered up when she recalled her conviction that they wouldn't get past the 'Good morning—Goodbye' stage; Nate would very soon be telling her 'On your bike'. And she pictured him then, that sour expression on his face, probably at this very moment seated in some plane anywhere between here and America, and didn't feel at all ashamed at the wish that entered her head, the wish that hoped he was a bad traveller and at the very least was prone to being airsick.

She left such delightful visions as her telephone shrilled for attention, and, part way to getting ready for bed, she shrugged into her housecoat prior to going to answer it.

Then she discovered that Nate Kingersby was not as she had hoped being ill on a bumpy flight. He had not yet taken off. For it was his in no way conciliatory voice that met her ears as briefly he gave his name and stated the reason for his call.

'I'm phoning from the hospital,' he told her tersely. And as though for himself he would rather expire than ask a favour of her, he grunted, 'Rex is very down. He's going demented wanting to see you.'

Discounting that Nate wasn't putting himself out to be

agreeable, having realised she didn't hate Rex as she would
have thought after what he had done, at that moment
Kathryn felt so sorry for her ex-fiancé that she almost said
she would pay him a visit. Then last Friday's scene flashed
into her head and again she felt nausea well up, a sickness
invading her that on many occasions Rex must have broken
faith with her.

'So?' she answered coolly, as other reminders came—
memories of her heartbroken mother, of Sandra heading the
same way.

'So,' Nate said, aggression only just beneath the surface,
'are you going to visit him?'

'You're asking me?' she questioned, playing for time,
trying to remember what the ward Sister had told her a short
while ago. Hadn't she said depression was usual in a case
like Rex's? That he would probably be over it by tomorrow?

Her question was met by a long silence. Then for all he
was sounding nowhere near as if ready to plead with her, she
heard Nate, his tones even, say:

'Yes, I'm asking you. Begging if you like. Please will you
go and see him?'

Her decision was made before he finished. And it was
most likely nerves, brought on by the fact that she knew
Nate Kingersby would turn ugly when she acquainted
him with it, that had her bringing out a light laugh that
she saw afterwards he had interpreted as a scoffing
laugh.

'It's not like you to beg, is it, Nate?' And getting in there
quickly before he could fire, 'You're wasting my time and
yours—I have no intention of visiting Rex.' She could
almost feel the crackle of ice travelling up the wires as she
added, only just getting in before him, 'Surely even you
didn't imagine my small supply of decency would extend
that far?'

'You *bitch*!' greeted her ears in unconcealed fury. 'You

callous, coldhearted bitch! I'll get even with you for this if it takes me . . .'

Kathryn put down the phone. She had heard enough. Her hands were shaking as she collapsed into a chair, his words ringing threateningly in her ears. Of course she knew why he was mad. He had lowered himself so far as to tell her he was ready to beg on his brother's behalf—and what had she done but laughed scoffingly at him?

What had made her do it? Again he had had that effect on her of making her react entirely opposite from her real nature. She could just as easily have explained, in a nice way, that she didn't want to be engaged to Rex, that she thought if she paid him a visit Rex would gather from that that things were back to the way they were between them.

He wouldn't have believed her anyway, she thought a few moments later. He hadn't credited her with any finer feelings from the beginning. He certainly wouldn't believe it had she told him she was afraid seeing Rex bed-bound and bandaged might have her agreeing to continuing being engaged to him just to aid his recovery.

Why was she getting so stewed up over the Kingersbys anyway? she wondered, getting up from her chair and going to put the kettle on for a warm drink. Rex couldn't have loved her as much as he'd vowed he did in the first place— not if he could carry on the way he had with his secretary behind her back.

Kathryn was glad to feel her spirit returning as she pottered about in the kitchen. Why should she bother about Nate Kingersby either? His threats didn't mean a thing. He couldn't harm her. The worst he could do was dismiss her, and that would suit her fine. It was just lovely to her way of thinking, because if the instruction came from Nate for her to leave, then she couldn't possibly be accused of breaking her promise to his uncle, could she?

As she had anticipated, the rest of the week turned out to

be very busy. Though on Friday when she was taking dictation the phone rang and Erica Naisby, secretary to Jeremy Kingersby who managed Insurance, told her she had called through to remind her she was leaving that day and not to forget the lunchtime session in the Crown—a long-standing custom in the firm on anyone's last day.

Kathryn had forgotten, but hadn't anything else planned. 'Wouldn't miss it, Erica. I'll be over just after one,' she told her, then put down the phone and explained to George what the interruption had been about.

'We'd better get as much done as we can this morning,' he cracked, 'if you're going to be tipsy this afternoon!'

She grinned. He had never seen her tipsy yet, and at the most a couple of gin and tonics were all she intended imbibing. Though she did work hard for the rest of the morning just in case her concentration was not a hundred per cent that afternoon.

By the time she was free to go over to the Crown, it was ten past one, and just by following her ears, sounds reminiscent of a parrot house mixing with gusts of laughter, she was able to find the crowd from the office.

She was greeted by several people, one or two passing sympathetic comments about Rex's accident and the fact that the wedding tomorrow had had to be put off—and she just couldn't then tell any of them that her engagement had been broken.

Though when Erica pushed her way through the crush and asked her what she was drinking she noticed she was no longer wearing her ring. Kathryn mumbled something about it being, 'Just one of those things,' and warmed to Erica, who had once been engaged herself but who had never got to the altar, when she commented:

'Better to find out before than after. Gin and tonic right?'

The next half an hour flew by in snatches of conversation

and wisecracks. But it was as Kathryn stood for a moment chatting to one of the men from the Insurance department that Jeremy Kingersby came in. She had a smile on her lips ready with some form of greeting, for she and Rex had once or twice gone out with Jeremy and his wife in a foursome. But to her astonishment, her 'Hello, Jeremy,' was absolutely ignored as he nodded a greeting to the man from his department, then turned his back on her.

Her astonishment must have been showing, because it brought forth the comment from her companion, 'He couldn't have heard you in all this racket.'

But Kathryn knew differently. She had realised, too late to go in for any ignoring herself, that Jeremy knew she had thrown Rex over, and being a true Kingersby, had refused to acknowledge her.

It had been what she had been expecting, she told herself, finding her gin and tonic of the utmost interest. George, whom the years had mellowed and who knew her better than any of them apart from Rex, hadn't ignored her, though, she thought, just before a half remembered memory came of her standing with a clutch of other people waiting for the lift on Wednesday. Tim Kingersby, another of the cousins, had walked by and she had started to say hello, only he hadn't seen her, or so she thought. But with Jeremy cutting her just now, she was beginning to wonder.

By the time people began to drift back to their offices, Jeremy Kingersby having been near on a couple of occasions but deliberately not seeing her, Kathryn knew she should start looking for another job. Better start looking straight away too. Nate Kingersby, she didn't doubt, would take charge of Kingersby International at nine a.m. a week on Monday, and at one minute past nine precisely on that day he would take great delight in terminating her services with the company.

A week followed where every day she scanned the paper,

but saw nothing that held the interest for her that she found in her present job. Still, she wasn't in any hurry, she thought, as she started work on the last Friday she would be working for George Kingersby. She could afford to wait a month, maybe two, before her jobless situation became urgent.

Technically George was still chairman until after his holiday, until the jubilee celebrations were over. But slack as they were that Friday, everything they could think of having been cleared up, he was taking things easy on this his last day in harness.

It was about mid-afternoon that Kathryn tactfully closed the door between the two offices on her way out. It had crossed her mind that he might need a few moments of solitude while he finished gathering up his possessions accumulated over the years, that he might need a few minutes of privacy while he sat back and reflected how well those years had panned out, how all his hard work and that of his brothers, not to mention that of his sons and nephews, had made it the thriving business it was today.

She was in the middle of some typing when the door to the left of her was thrust unceremoniously open. Her eyes jerked to it, met hostile blue eyes, then went swiftly back to her typewriter. She hadn't expected to see *him* until next Monday, and then only briefly.

She heard him come to stand by her desk, but wouldn't look up. That was until she heard the nasty way he snarled:

'I thought you were leaving.'

Her colour rose, so did her temper. Unsmiling, she raised her head, lifted her eyes a long way up. Checking on the angry retort that wanted to have its head, she said sweetly:

'You're not the chairman yet,' and didn't miss the look on his face that savoured the moment when he was, the moment when he could tell her just where she could go.

Nor could she resist the most beautiful urge to try and make him change colour. 'As a matter of fact,' she said, syrup dripping, 'you might be interested to learn that your uncle made me promise to stay on and work for you for three months.'

She knew he was remembering the way she had broken her promise to marry his brother by the way his eyes iced over.

'And of course you never break your promises, do you?' he sneered.

'This is one I fully intend keeping,' she said for the pure hell of it—and got the devil's own shock to hear not the reply she was confident of hearing, but:

'Oh God! Have I got to put up with you for three months?'

Shaken rigid, Kathryn couldn't believe what she had heard. Surely he couldn't mean he would keep her on? She was sure, where he hadn't changed colour one iota, that she had gone pale. All pretended sweetness left her, at any rate, as she hurried to tell him:

'I made the promise to Mr Kingersby. Your uncle didn't promise me I could keep my job for three months.' There! She had more or less invited him to sack her. She waited. Even a hint that that was what he intended to do on Monday would have sufficed.

But no such hint came her way. And if her eyes weren't deceiving her there was a devilish gleam in Nate Kingersby's eyes as he read what she had been expecting.

'Should you ever get to know us Kingersbys sufficiently,' he drawled, that satanic gleam still there, 'then you'll learn, Miss Randle, that as a family we never break faith with each other. If my uncle has seen fit to exact such a promise from you, then let me assure you I'll keep you to it—no matter how diabolical I personally happen to consider the situation to be.'

With that, Kathryn only just managing to keep her mouth from sagging open, he turned and strode smartly through the other door. She heard George's happy cry of, 'Nate!' and then the door closed.

Lofty swine! she fumed, while her furious thoughts fought for precedence. Then, damn him, damn him! If she didn't want to be thought a girl who broke every promise she made at the drop of a hat, then wasn't she committed to working for that cocksure creature for three months?

Three whole months! she thought aghast. For hadn't he as good as said the Kingersby honour decreed that he couldn't dismiss her without making his first action in his role of chairman to break faith with his uncle the minute his back was turned?

Kathryn forgot about her typing and felt more like crying. Oh, why had she told Nate Kingersby about that promise? He had sworn to get even with her, and she had just handed him three long, long months in which to try!

CHAPTER FOUR

HAVING spent the weekend in coming to terms with what she saw was to be her lot for the next three months, Kathryn got out of bed on Monday morning wishing, not for the first time, that she could lose that something that was part of her make-up, decreeing that she couldn't break her promise to George Kingersby.

She had said goodbye to him on Friday, aware of the uselessness of wishing he wasn't going. He had smiled at her downcast expression, made her smile too on realising he wasn't too old not to feel flattered that losing him as her boss should make her look so upset.

'I'll be coming back,' he had teased. 'Wouldn't miss the celebrations for anything. And anyway, I'm leaving you in good hands, aren't I?'

If his reference to Nate taking his place had been designed to cheer her up, he very soon saw as her smile disappeared that it had had the opposite effect. George's smile too had vanished as he had quickly reminded her of her promise to him.

'You won't let me down, Kathryn, will you? You will stay on and give Nate all the assistance you can in these first three trying months?'

Sorely tempted to try and wriggle out of it, she had looked at the old workhorse, his need for a holiday evident, and had known then that with his high principles there was a very big chance that he would still cancel his holiday unless she re-affirmed her promise.

'Of course I'll stay,' she had said brightly. 'I've given you my word, haven't I?'

Coldhearted bitch, she thought, coming out of the bathroom. Oh, if only she was! She wouldn't now be preparing to don one of her best suits because her confidence needed a booster. She wouldn't have set her alarm for that half an hour earlier to make doubly sure she arrived on time and didn't get her first black mark of the day for being late.

Ready, and with time to spare, she stood in her bedroom in front of her full-length mirror running a critical eye over her appearance. Neatly polished brown leather shoes with a two-inch heel, comfortable though still leaving her about eight inches short of his height if Nate had any inclination— and she was sure he had—of looking down his nose at her today. She ousted him from her mind as her inspection continued. Sheer ten-denier tights, not at all practical for the office, but since her legs were slender and shapely with trim ankles she didn't see why she shouldn't go the whole hog on this confidence kick. Her suit was tobacco brown, a suit she'd bought to wear to the office after her marriage, thinking that as Mrs Kingersby she had better dress up to her name. She bit her lip at the unexpected catch in her throat at that thought, but knew it was only an unhealed nerve end from the time she had spent on untrustworthy dreams. The cream shirt she wore beneath her jacket went well with her creamy skin she thought.

Staying only to check that the small amount of make-up she used didn't need further attention, and wishing her delicate-looking nose was sharper so that if she caught Nate Kingersby sitting down she might have the chance of looking arrogantly down it at him, she snatched up her bag and made for her Mini.

Her plans had worked out well. She was early arriving at Kingersby International. Now to get to her office, to be hard at it when the new chairman came in. She might glance up when he came through the door, she considered, might flick him a cool good morning with her eyes and then carry on with her work as though this morning wasn't any different from any other morning. She might . . .

Her plans backfired the moment she opened her office door. Nate Kingersby was there before her. She saw him through the dividing door the minute she went in, a door that looked to have been purposely left open. So he's watching to see what time I arrive, she thought, mutinous before she started. Then realising this was no way to begin a three-month stint that would probably find release in fireworks before the week was out, she threw an insincere smile in his direction.

'Good morning,' she said politely, and discovered Nate Kingersby wasn't the sort of man who went in for smiles, insincere or otherwise, and wondered why she had bothered as even her greeting wasn't returned.

'Come through when you've sorted yourself out,' he said abruptly. And so started her day.

Kathryn hadn't dragged her feet when she had worked for George, she mused as wearily that night she drove home. Though with him she had occasionally stopped while they came up for air, stopped and passed a pleasantry or two which helped the day along.

But not one pleasantry had Nate Kingersby dropped her way. And as for coming up for air, he just didn't seem to need it. And so much for George thinking he would need her help to see him through this transitional stage. Not once had Nate Kingersby asked her advice. He had seen at a glance, it appeared, what needed to be done, and had got right in there and done it. And very early in the day she had learned that Nate Kingersby was a demon for work.

She had her meal, her mind going over the problems he had handled with consummate ease that day, the telephone calls he had dealt with, showing her he had a wealth of charm at his disposal when he chose to use it when one irate customer had rung through and insisted on speaking only with the chairman if they didn't want to lose his account over some foul-up or other of the kind that occasionally happened in big business.

She couldn't doubt then, when Nate had had their client positively purring at the end of the conversation, that the right man had been chosen for the job—even if it did mean she had never worked so hard in her life. She paused, wondering if every day was going to be as hectic as this one. The idea came—had Nate been working her so hard her fingers felt typed down to the stumps from the pure dislike he felt for her, hoping she would quit; or was he testing her to see just how good she was?

It was food for thought. She and Rex had started going out with each other within the first week of her working at Kingersby International. Word had soon got round about it. And with the Kingersby clan being so one for all, all for one, wouldn't it be natural for Nate to wonder if she was up to the job she had been taken on to do? Couldn't he be thinking, since she and Rex had very soon grown serious about each other, that she had been kept on in the job from some sort of nepotism?

Kathryn went to bed still chewing the matter over, and got up the next morning refreshed from sleeping the sleep of the exhausted and on her mettle to prove she was up to handling the job she had been taken on to do. She knew she was capable, had proved it to George without the need to examine her conscience. But if Nate Kingersby wanted proof she would show him again today, as she had yesterday, that Kathryn Randle could cope with anything he threw her way, if not exactly standing on her head, then without any signs of flagging.

'Good morning,' she offered as she went in, prepared this time to see him seated behind his desk. Though this time she didn't bother with her insincere smile.

This morning her greeting was answered, for all it was more in the nature of a grunt. We're coming on, she thought without humour, pausing only to drop her bag. She went through the open door, leaving it open, since Nate had objected yesterday when she had closed it. If he wanted to keep tabs on her, she decided, he could get on with it. She was wearing the same suit she had worn yesterday, though today she had teamed it with a sage green shirt.

Nate motioned her to the chair she normally used to take dictation, saying not a word as his eyes took in her appearance, her neat cap of dark brown hair shining healthily, his eyes flicking to the contours outlined beneath her fitting jacket. And for all his inspection of her was cursory, Kathing felt the warm pink colour in her cheeks as his eyes rested on her breasts.

Of course he had to catch her blush, and she could have hit him at the sardonic look that came over his face—a look that clearly told her that when it came to his fancying women she wouldn't get a look in.

'Whatever is going through your sweet little mind,' his hard words endorsed his look, 'forget it. I'm here to work. Just remember—so are you.' And just as though he thought she had him next in line on her list of suitable males, he infuriated her by adding, 'If it's in your mind to try and add me to your collection of wounded suitors, perhaps you'll take note that I regard one broken member in any family as more than sufficient. Added to which, I like my women with some semblance of a heart.'

'Why, you egotistical swine!' shot from her without thought, without the slightest regard for his position in the company. 'I'd as soon fancy a gorilla as fancy you! And for your information, the only reason I blushed just now is because I'm not used to men mentally stripping me.' It was an exaggeration, she knew it, for his eyes hadn't lingered that long, but she was too worked up to pick and choose her words.

'Of course,' he drawled coolly, insufferably unaffected by her accusation, 'You're more used to men physically stripping you. aren't you?'

'You . . .' she started to explode, only to find he had chopped her off by reaching for his briefcase, extracting some files and saying:

'See what sense you can make of that little lot.'

That little lot took her up to eleven. He must have worked well into the night, she thought, trying to make sense out of his rapid scrawl, for all his figures were neatly compiled. She typed back the several letters he had drafted in his abbreviated longhand while the context of the correspondence was fresh in his mind, but was still fuming when she took her work through to him and had to sit while he dictated more.

It was during the afternoon that it came to her, as she considered how the time had flown, that either she was enjoying working for Nate or her anger with him had got her through a tremendous amount that day. Her back gave a twinge from sitting in the same position for so long, and she leaned back in her chair, her jacket long since dispensed with, and caught Nate's eyes on her. For the briefest of moments those blue eyes were so without hostility, admiring almost—though whether because she had kept up with him throughout the day or from the view he had of her from where he was sitting she couldn't have said—but that hostility for the first time had gone, and her own fury with him suddenly disappeared.

Without thinking, a friendly smile winged from her, the sort of smile she would have sent his uncle in their moments of coming up for air. Instantly she regretted it. Nate's dark brow came down, and she couldn't doubt that hostility was back in full force.

'Have you finished that report?' he grated, when he knew full well she hadn't since it was still in her typewriter, she thought, wondering how good her aim would be if she dared hurl her stapler at him.

'Miracles take a little longer,' she flung instead, and crashed into her typewriter again.

Thank God for Friday, she thought as she dragged herself out of bed on Friday morning. For she had come round to thinking that Nate Kingersby must sleep plugged into an electric charger. Not once this week had he let up, but had kept her shoulder pressed firmly to the wheel—so firmly she had begun to think he was looking for work to try and wear her down. For George had left things more or less up to date when he had departed, and though new problems cropped up ever day, never had there been a week like this one.

Still, Kathryn thought, determined not to go under, she had Saturday and Sunday to look forward to. She'd have a lie in tomorrow, then start doing something about getting back into circulation again. Perhaps she'd ring up one of her girl friends and see if anyone fancied going to the cinema.

But any ideas on how she was going to spend her weekend were doomed to failure when at four that afternoon, when she happened to be in Nate's office, the phone on her desk rang.

'Take it in here,' he ordered without looking up from the typed matter she had put in front of him.

It wouldn't have taken a couple of seconds for her to nip to her desk, but thinking it would be someone asking to be put through to him anyway, Kathryn did as she was instructed. And on hearing her sister's distraught voice promptly she forgot everything save that Sandra sounded in deep distress and needed her.

'Calm down, love, do,' she urged, her suspicion that

Victor was up to his old tricks again proving to be only too true.

'How can I calm down?' Sandra wailed. 'Vic's just been home and packed a bag saying his firm are holding a weekend seminar in Birmingham!'

'Well, they could be,' she said, not believing it for a moment, not with Victor Smith anyway.

'They do sometimes, I know,' Sandra admitted, and then bursting into tears, 'But I followed him upstairs when he went to change and there was—was lipstick on his shirt!'

The rotter! Kathryn thought, oblivious to the fact Nate Kingersby had finished with the paper work she had given him and wasn't above tuning into her end of the conversation.

'Are you sure?' she questioned. Her heart went out to Sandra, but there was a coldness gripping her that there were such men around. 'It might not have been lipstick.'

She knew she was saying all the things Sandra wanted to hear, things she herself knew to be false. But Sandra wouldn't throw him out anyway, and if it eased things for her she loved her enough to stamp down on the urge to tell her to kick him out.

'He works in an office, doesn't he? I'm always going home smothered in red felt tip.' It was a lie, but Sandra was desperate for consolation.

'Oh, Kathryn,' she wept, 'I don't know what I'll do if he leaves me!'

Kathryn had to fight hard not to tell her sister she was ten times too good for the rat of a man she had married, that she was the one who should leave him.

'Don't cry, Sandy,' she said, feeling helpless. 'Look, there's only another hour to go before I leave work. You can fix me up with some gear if I drive to you straight from the office, can't you?'

'Would you?' Already Sandra was beginning to sound more stable. 'You'll stay the weekend? If—if Vic doesn't . . .' she started to cry again. 'If he doesn't come home on S-Sunday . . .'

'Of course he'll come home on Sunday,' Kathryn said bracingly, sure of it. He knew which side his bread was buttered, didn't he?

In the process of making more soothing noises, she became aware suddenly of where she was. Her eyes flew to where Nate Kingersby should have been checking over the typed list of figures she had brought it. Only he wasn't. His eyes were fixed on her, her conversation apparently of the greatest interest. Trust him, she thought, to take this precise moment to decide a couple of minutes' rest wouldn't come amiss.

'I'll have to go now, Sandra,' she said, not wanting to cut her sister short but now aware of an unwanted pair of ears, her feelings of being natural deserting her. 'I'll get to you the minute I can.'

Emotionally out of her stride as she was by the repugnance she felt at this latest escapade of her sister's husband, it helped not at all to know that Nate Kingersby had had an ear cocked to her call. But she tried to look ready to resume work.

Assuming he had finished checking the figures she had placed in front of him, she leaned across to retrieve them. Then was halted by hearing him address her for the first time since Tuesday with a remark that had nothing to do with work.

'If memory serves,' he said, with the attitude of a man trying to dredge up some half listened to information from somewhere, 'your *sister*'s name is Sandra, isn't it?'

'That's right,' she acknowledged briefly, having to pull her hand away from the papers and stand back when he leaned forward his arm clipping them down so she couldn't catch hold of her neat piece of work without ripping it.

'Does one gather from the lipstick-stroke-red felt tip-festooned garment that your sister has a philandering husband?'

You can gather what the devil you like, Kathryn wanted to tell him. But that word 'philandering' hit at the very heart of her. And, her emotions already out of hand, her face paled, her eyes taking a wounded look.

'It's sick,' she said, trying to get back on an even keel but not making a very good job of it as she exclaimed bitterly, 'How Sandra can live with such a man . . .!' She broke off. She didn't want Nate knowing any of her private business. 'I—I'm sorry,' she apologised, more for bringing something other than business into the office than anything else, for all it was he who had carried on where her phone call had left off by asking his questions. 'It's just . . .' How to explain the bitterness in her that must have come across? 'It's just that if there's one thing that gets through to me,' she had to continue, thoughts of her father joining on her sister's husband, 'it's infidelity.'

'Infidelity!'

It was his turn to exclaim, and there was a touch of bitterness in his voice too. A bitterness Kathryn was too involved in the suffering of her female relative to understand as meaning he was bitter on account of the infidelity served to his male kin.

'Yes,' she said, 'infidelity. Just the word makes me curl up inside.'

The words had barely left her before his, 'Like hell it does!' rudely assaulted her ears.

Shaken out of her thoughts, still desperately trying to get back to being the cool secretary she had been before Sandra's phone call had thrown her, Kathryn just looked at him.

'What do you mean?' she asked.

And that was too much for Nate and his anger. He was on his feet, towering over her, a cynical disbelieving look there in his eyes blazing as he rammed home:

'So much do you prize *fidelity* that while still engaged to my brother you had arrangements made for an illicit weekend!' Kathryn's brown eyes went enormous, but while still dazed from his thundering attack, he was going on, 'How long was it after you broke with Rex before you slipped away with your next conquest to a place where no one could find you? Ten minutes—an hour? Or was . . .'

'I didn't go away with anyone,' she defended hotly, swiftly coming round.

'So you say,' he bit at her, the scornful look in his eyes telling her he thought every word she uttered was suspect.

But she had grown angry enough not to be bothered by his cynical disbelieving look anyway. 'I didn't,' she repeated stormily. 'For your information, I went *by myself* to stay with Sandra in Reading.'

'Why?' The question came promptly. 'Was her husband away philandering that time too?'

His sarcasm grated. 'No,' she answered, seething. 'For once he was at home.' Anger suddenly vanished as that remembered weekend, that time when all her emotions had seemed frozen solid, came back to her. 'It wasn't Sandra who was upset. It was me.'

Her words had left her quietly, her eyes clouded with memories of those numbed hours after she had discovered Rex's deception. And all at once in the taut silence that followed she had the oddest notion that now she wasn't charging full pelt to vindicate herself, but by admitting in the quiet way she had that she was upset, Nate Kingersby looked more as if he gave credence to anything she had to say than he had ever done.

'You were upset?' he queried, his eyes narrowing.

'Yes, I was,' she said, still quietly.

Then she saw it was only for a brief while that he had looked ready to give credit that she might be speaking the truth. For in seconds he had come up with his own reckoning of why she had been disturbed in any way.

'You would be upset, wouldn't you?' he agreed, and there was nothing pleasant in the way he said it. 'With *fidelity* ranking so highly with you it had come to you after you'd broken your engagement that you'd just said goodbye to the one man you could count on never abusing your trust.'

'Count on!' she echoed, staggered, knowing she could floor him in one go if she . . . 'How do you know I could count so wholeheartedly on Rex's faithfulness?' she couldn't resist demanding.

She received a look of fury that she should dare to challenge his brother's integrity. Nate controlled his fury— just. And it was then that Kathryn found herself on the receiving end of his high and mighty arrogance.

'I know,' he told her, looking down from his lofty height, 'because there's a trait common to all Kingersby men, a trait that while it extends to some of them being a bit wild beforehand, means that once a Kingersby has given his heart, other women cease to exist.'

She couldn't help the jeering laugh that left her. Rex must be a throwback, then—or he had never loved her as much as he had claimed.

'You dare to doubt it?' The hold Nate had had on his fury was leaving, she could see it by the way his jaw jutted, and she didn't need many guesses to know her jeering laugh had been instrumental in giving it a hand. Then he was in charge of his temper, arrogant again as he sneered, 'Of course you doubt it,' and contemptuously, 'Never having given your heart to my brother in the first place you would have no idea of the feeling, would you?'

Anger beset her again that he could make so light of the feeling she had had for Rex before his actions had killed it.

'I did give my heart,' she flared.

'Oh, sure. You gave it so unreservedly that even when I told you he was going demented wanting to see you, you laughed as you threw my plea to go and see him back in my face.' She knew it galled him that he had ever been ready to beg her to do anything as he snarled, 'And now you're trying to tell me you love him?'

'Since you don't intend to believe anything I say it's pointless telling you anything, isn't it?' she said coldly— then found, having no clear idea why, because Nate was so dead set against her and careless of any explanation she made anyway, that she wanted him to understand why she hadn't been able to go and visit his brother. 'Don't you see,' she tried, 'that in all honesty I couldn't go and see him? Not if—not if, as you seem to think, Rex still believes he cares for me.'

'You're still afraid you might find yourself tied up to a cripple?'

'You said he wouldn't be a permanent invalid,' she retorted, knowing she was wasting her time arguing since he only ever interpreted anything she said the wrong way. 'What I'm trying to make you see is that having broken with him I might—I was afraid I might find myself engaged to him again.'

'Your soft little heart,' he jibed sarcastically, making her want to hit out at him.

Then all at once his face darkened, and suddenly she was experiencing fear. For a dreadful cold light had come to his eyes, and Kathryn knew then that for all he continued in that same hateful sarcastic way, Nate Kingersby wanted his revenge for what she had done to his brother.

'You've had practice in breaking your engagement before,' he continued to jibe. 'Practice in breaking my brother's heart.' A muscle moved near his temple as his eyes pierced her. 'Surely that practice would have stood you in good stead had your *tenderhearted* feelings at seeing him temporarily helpless had you wearing his ring once more.'

That hellbent revengeful look was still there in his cold, hating face. It made her afraid to move, to speak, chilled her to the marrow. Nate had said he meant to get even with her, and suddenly she knew without him repeating that threat that most of this conversation was designed to get whatever information he could from her. Information he would use against her at a later date.

'Why did you jilt my brother a week before the wedding?' he asked while she was trying frantically hard not to believe he intended to do her the greatest harm he could. 'That is if you're to be believed and there was no other man.'

Kathryn looked into eyes that didn't try to hide their merciless light. She knew then if she so much as dared to tell the truth it would augur ill for her, that he would add what she said to the list of lies he thought she had already told him. Add that to everything he had against her—all to be harvested on the day he had his reckoning with her. She remembered his hands around her throat . . .

'Hasn't Rex told you?' She backed away from telling him the truth.

'He's still believing you're the sweetest woman ever to have been created,' he told her icily—then let her know he considered Rex to be fairer than lilywhite in the broken engagement. 'He's not likely to blacken your name by giving details of your last meeting, is he? You might think about that the next time you start to get uptight at that word fidelity.' Her nerves ragged, she flinched at that word 'fidelity', and saw the light that suddenly came to his eyes. 'My brother's—fidelity—to you is without question,' he said, deliberately using that word a second time, she thought, involuntarily flinching again. And she had the strangest notion then that that word had sealed an idea that had been forming in Nate Kingersby's mind ever since this conversation had got started.

Trying to get on top of her fear, the wild hallucinating of her mind that he was plotting anything in any way evil for her, Kathryn brought up her reserves of courage and decided then and there that if he was still waiting to hear why, as he termed it, she had jilted his brother, then he could jolly well wait. She had had enough of his sarcasm, his jibes, his downright disbelief of anything she told him, without inviting any more of all three by telling him the truth.

She looked past him to the document on his desk he had checked through, then without saying another word she leaned across, picked it up and went smartly back to her desk. And there she tried for actions that had come to her naturally before those words 'fidelity' and 'infidelity' had been bandied about in the other room. Calmer now, she realised she had let her imagination go almost hysterically wild in there. Nate Kingersby didn't seem nearly so threatening now she was back in her own office.

Her mind turned to Sandra with her faithless husband and she checked her watch. Half past four. Poor Sandra! Only another half an hour and she could leave the office, leave despicable Nate Kingersby, and be on her way to be of what comfort she could to her sister. With luck Sandra would feel better tomorrow. And the idea took root, for dismissing her fears that her boss might still have plans to finish what had seemed likely in her flat and maybe strangle her as being all part of her overwrought imagination at the time, that she didn't know how much more of him she could take, so perhaps some time this weekend she might have a few moments when she could get to grips with the thought that was looming large—could she live with her conscience if she broke her promise to George Kingersby and gave in her notice on Monday?

'Leave that.'

Kathryn looked up startled from what she was doing. Startled not so much that Nate had so soon followed her into her office, but that amazingly there was not an atom of aggression in his voice. He had changed in the space of a few minutes from the entirely disagreeable character he had been, and now, if appearances were to be believed, was being the most affable she had ever seen him.

'Leave it?' she queried, not trusting him, wary too of the smile he suddenly sent her way. A smile, for her! Never had she seen him smile before. It made his good-looking face light up, showed strong even teeth, and she just couldn't believe in it. Not after the way he had been.

'We were both a bit—uptight in there,' he explained, causing her almost to gasp as the possibility struck that he might be apologising for the brute he had been. 'Me with my thoughts centred on my brother—you with your thoughts, feelings, all wrapped up with your sister and her husband's lack of fidelity.'

That word again! Had it been used deliberately to probe her reaction, for reacted she had in the quick shuttering of her eyes before she stared at him again. But this time the sick feeling that word awakened didn't linger as once more a smile curved Nate's well constructed mouth.

'It occurred to me,' he remarked, with such charm it left her blinking, 'that if we're to continue working together, and since neither of us wants to break faith with my uncle, then we must—we ought to be grown up enough to bury the bone of contention that's between us during working hours. Wouldn't you agree?'

The pure charm of him had her forgetting she had been hoping to find the courage this weekend to ignore her promise to his uncle and give in her notice on Monday.

'You've worked wonderfully well this week,' Nate went on. 'Come out on top no matter how hard I've pressed you.

Will you forgive the bear I've been and start afresh with me on Monday?'

'I . . .' Kathryn struggled. She felt flattered that her hard work had not gone unnoticed, but she just couldn't believe in this complete turn-around coming so quickly after what had so recently gone on in his office.

'I know I haven't given you an easy time,' Nate went on, his face serious now, which gave her to think either he was being very sincere or was by way of being a very good actor. 'But I hope my attitude hasn't caused you to think in terms of breaking your promise to my uncle.'

'Good heavens, no,' Kathryn lied quickly, and was on the receiving end of that charm, that smile again, as he extended his hand.

'Fresh start on Monday, then, Kathryn?' he asked.

Without her being fully aware of it her hand came out. She felt it taken in his large firm hand. 'Yes, all right,' she heard herself say. Then she had to feel he was being sincere when he dropped her hand and told her:

'I know you're anxious to get to your sister as quickly as possible. Leave everything, I'll clear up your desk for you.'

'You'll clear . . .!'

'Go now,' he said, part charm, part authoritative. Then, pleasantly, 'Enjoy what you can of the weekend.'

Kathryn's head was buzzing as she reversed her car out of the car park. Had that really happened? The feel of his warm clasp as solemnly he had shaken hands was still with her—so it must have happened!

But away from his charm, his overpowering presence, she just had to ask—why? Only a few minutes earlier he had been ready to flatten her had she uttered one word against his brother. Yet very shortly afterwards he was suggesting they forget all about Rex while they were at work in the interests of working harmoniously together!

She negotiated traffic automatically as she puzzled on this

latest development. Whether the atmosphere in the office
was harmonious or otherwise wouldn't bother him in the
slightest, she was sure about that. So why had he changed
so totally—and in such a very brief space of time?

She had seen him make a few lightning decisions this
week. She knew he was capable of rapid thought, rapid and
unfaltering summing up; so what thoughts had come to him
that had had him rapidly changing from a man who looked
so darkly threatening that her imagination had run riot, to
a man who suddenly professed that harmony in the office
was his first consideration—when she knew that it wasn't?

Kathryn was nearly in Reading before she had the
answer—the only answer that would fit, anyway, since
Nate had spoken of their burying their bone of contention
during working hours, and since she wasn't likely to be
meeting him out of working hours that was all she had to
worry about. It had to be, didn't it, that unnoticed by her
he must have been observing her while she was contemplat-
ing the possibility of leaving before her three months were
up? He was shrewd, was Nate. He must have caught some
fleeting expression on her face that told him she was
thinking of breaking her promise to his uncle. She had seen
an honesty in him this week in his business dealings and
saw then that since George was bound to ask the question
when he returned of why had she left, Nate would have to
confess, with that same honesty, that it had been his
attitude with her that had driven her out. He had said
something about keeping faith with his uncle when she had
all but invited him to dismiss her, hadn't he? Wasn't
driving her out tantamount to his breaking faith with his
uncle?

Almost on Sandra's doorstep, she realised she had better
forget about work and concentrate on how best to help her
sister. She knew from past experience that to suggest as
she had after Victor's first escapade—the first one Sandra

had found out about anyway—that advising her to call it a day with him was not the way to make her sister feel any better. Sandra had rushed to his defence then, and seeing it was she who was married to him, ever after that Kathryn had bitten her tongue on what she would like to have said, and spent her energies on being what support she could in the many times Sandra had suffered afterwards. She had the experience of the support they had both given her mother to draw on—support she had given before a bout of 'flu, neglected while she had been away from her on holiday, had turned to pneumonia and killed her. She had died the day she had returned, Kathryn remembered—and remembered also the way her father, beside himself with grief at the time, had remarried very shortly afterwards. Her teeth clenched, Kathryn didn't doubt that the second Mrs Randle was being cheated.

'You're sooner than I expected.' Sandra rushed out to greet her, her red eyes showing that her tears hadn't ended with their telephone conversation, though Kathryn was pleased to see she appeared to be brighter than she had sounded then.

'My boss thought he'd worked me hard enough this week,' she said lightly. 'He told me I could go early.'

The weekend that followed was not memorable for its joy. Sandra returned to the subject of her husband whenever Marigold and Gillie were not in earshot. And Kathryn didn't have to recall how wonderful her sister had been to her a couple of weeks ago when her own world had fallen apart to listen again and again, withholding any sharp comment on hearing Sandra's hopefully declared thoughts that once the frequently erring Vic had got his womanising out of his system he would settle down to being a model husband.

She hid, successfully she hoped, the nausea she felt when he breezed in just after eight on Sunday night and presented his wife with a box of chocolates. She swallowed down her feeling of wanting to be physically ill when he even had the audacity to ask his wife if she had missed him.

Since they hadn't had any idea when he would arrive, Kathryn had been going to stay again that night and drive back in the morning. But seeing the way Sandra was so pathetically grateful that he had thought of her long enough to buy her a box of chocolates made her so cross she wasn't sure she would be able to keep from giving him a piece of her mind should she be left alone with him for very long.

'I think I'll go home tonight,' she stated abruptly, not apologising for breaking in on the tale she could tell from his shifty-eyed look he was inventing on something one of the other 'fellows' had done yesterday.

'You weren't going to go until the morning,' Sandra began to protest.

'I know, love. But my new boss is mustard, I told you that. I think I'll be much more on my toes if I have only a short drive to work in the morning.'

'Fancy him, do you?' her brother-in-law had to put in his two pennyworth.

Kathryn hadn't been going to answer him. But just then Gillie called down from upstairs and Sandra left the room to go hurrying to her. 'With some men,' she said, finding she was too human after all to resist the dig, 'you know exactly where you are. Nate Kingersby, I have every confidence, would never let a woman think he loved her and then play her false.'

She drove home without regretting her remark. Victor Smith could have taken it that she was referring to Rex, but that thick her sister's husband wasn't.

Though as she drove along she couldn't help but wonder why she had drawn Nate Kingersby into it. And it irritated her too that she found herself remembering the Kingersby trait he had told her of, and wondering if he had ever told one particular woman that he loved her. He wasn't married, she knew that. Had he loved and lost? Or was he still waiting for that all-consuming passion he avowed so stoutly took the Kingersby men but once in a lifetime?—And why the heck should she bother her head about him and his love life anyway?

CHAPTER FIVE

DETERMINED to be early that second Monday in her role as secretary to Nate Kingersby, Kathryn slept late, rushed around her flat getting ready, then found her car had chosen that particular morning to go temperamental on her.

After much coaxing followed by a few sharp words she eventually got it going, but knew she was going to be fifteen minutes late. It would look well if Nate had changed back to the person he had been, she fretted, as hurriedly she parked the Mini and with more speed than dignity entered the Kingersby International building. He had been watching every minute last week to pounce on her for the smallest mistake. What if he reverted to being the way he had been? Oh lord, what a way to start the week! To fall foul of him before the week began.

Breathlessly she pushed open her office door, her eyes meeting arctic blue ones as she searched and found Nate seated in his office—and she knew the worst. Those few moments of him being amicable on Friday had been pure pretence. She knew it with certainty. For those frigid blue eyes looked back, telling her their owner hated her.

Her heart beating hurriedly, she lowered her eyes and went forward. Well, at least she would endeavour to be civil no matter what venom he had been storing up in the fifteen minutes he had been waiting for her to put in an appearance.

'I'm sorry I'm late,' she said, no warmth in her tones since she knew he was about to bite her head off, and having no intention of backing down before the fight began.

'Think nothing of it,' she heard him say, the vitriol she had been expecting nowhere to be heard.

74

It startled her into looking at him where before she had addressed her apology in his general direction. And she was suddenly stupefied to see that the hate she imagined she had read in his eyes was not there at all. That was what it was— pure imagination, she realised, as he smiled at her, taking in her trim figure in her hastily donned grey suit with its pink wool shirt. Imagination pure and simple, because she had been expecting a few short and to the point words. She had been several yards away when she thought she had read hate there for her, but close up there was nothing but that same bury-the-hatchet look he had given her on Friday.

'I expect you've had a fraught weekend,' he allowed her, still a suggestion of a smile curving his warm looking mouth.

'It—was rather,' she agreed, her own mouth starting to curve. 'Though to be honest I overslept, and then the car wouldn't start.'

'Well, you're here now,' Nate said tolerantly. 'When you've caught your breath we'll make a start, shall we?'

By the paper work covering his desk it looked as though he had already done half a day's work, but Kathryn didn't comment on it, feeling only relief that he *had* meant what he had said late on Friday afternoon.

So charming was Nate to her all through that day, Kathryn couldn't help but think that if there wasn't the ghost of Rex between them, she would love to have been his secretary for longer than the three months she had promised George. Oh, he still kept her hard at it, but he gave the work they did life. George had been good at his job too, but with Nate there were none of those temporary vague moments when the older man occasionally lost track of what they were doing and would remark, 'Where were we, Kathryn?'

She went home that night wondering how she had ever thought Nate Kingersby the most hateful man she had ever met, wondering why she had ever felt alarm at his threat to

get even with her. She was even able to realise his threat
had been made in temper and that people very often said
things in temper that they didn't really mean. But alone in
her flat, the charm of him that day not there to keep
memories at bay of how vile he had been to her in the past,
she was forced to pause and think again—was it all as
genuine as it seemed?

Could any man change so quickly from a man who had
looked ready to step over her unconcerned if she'd fallen
dead at his feet, to the man who that morning had waved
away her apology for being late—even suggest an excuse
for her lateness she hadn't offered in the weekend she had
just spent with Sandra? And could she trust him not to
return equally quickly to being the coldhearted fiend he had
been?

By Friday she knew that she could. She had just spent one
of the most stimulating weeks of her working career. Not
once had a sour note entered. Even working hard Nate had
still found time to treat her with charm and courtesy.

And if occasionally she looked through the door he still
liked to keep open between their two offices and caught him
looking at her, his eyes appearing hard, arctic and hating,
she knew the moment he threw her that half curving smile
before he bent to his work again that the distance that
divided them, a shadow that caught his face, had created
that erroneous impression. For there was no hate in his face
the few times he had come to see her with a query, or the
times he had called her in to take dictation or some other
matter.

'I want to leave early tonight,' he told her, and charm
again warmed her. 'You've slaved for me this week,
Kathryn, I don't think anyone would mind if you sloped off
early too.'

Why she should wonder where he was going that night
that he should be leaving early, she couldn't think. It was no

concern of hers if he had a heavy date. And she felt distinctly annoyed with herself that she should feel an odd sort of relief as the thought came that he probably intended to spend a longer time visiting Rex than usual.

At four o'clock she raised her head from what she was doing, caught what looked to be hostile eyes on her, and not waiting for the smile she was sure was to come, got her smile in first—and then felt her heart set up a very definite clamouring. For her smile was noted with a frown only a brief second before the most genuine smile she had ever received from him winged its way to her, just as though he couldn't help himself. It was gone instantly as he stood up, his face hidden as he bent his head momentarily.

Tearing her eyes from him, wondering at the clamouring inside her, Kathryn heard his voice, strangely cool coming from his room. 'We'll wrap it up for today.' And when she glanced through, she saw he was already clearing his desk ready for a fresh start on Monday.

She was just putting the cover on her typewriter when he came from his office, the briefcase in his hand denoting that if he had any idle hours between now and then he could find something to fill them with. But his voice had returned to being the same he had used all week when he asked:

'Anything planned for this weekend?'

How ridiculous, she thought moments later after quieting a heart that had rushed on the oddest notion that Nate was about to ask her out. Would he be likely to, with his brother, the man he thought she had jilted without cause, still confined to his hospital bed through drinking himself senseless when she'd handed him back his ring?

'Nothing special,' she replied, trying for a casual note. 'I shall probably go to the cinema—with a girl friend.' Why had she added that last bit? Good grief, was she seeking his good opinion? Was it that she wanted him to know that she wasn't an 'off with the old love, on with the new'? As if he'd care who she went to the pictures with!

He smiled at her, the smile she was growing used to, the smile that lightened his face that was so often gravely serious. 'I'll walk to the car park with you,' he announced, opening the door and standing back to let her go in front of him.

Kathryn was glad to reach the car park. She had been overwhelmingly conscious of him in the lift, had searched her mind for something to say, something to break the silence she suddenly felt stifling, for all it didn't seem to be affecting him. But she could think of nothing save to ask him how Rex was getting on, and some second sense was warning her that to bring his name up now, when it hadn't been mentioned all week, might have the week ending with her seeing some of Nate's aggression that had so far been absent.

She stumbled coming out of the lift, which didn't surprise her considering she suddenly felt as if she'd got two left feet. But Nate's hand came out swiftly, automatically, and prevented her from going headlong.

'Thanks,' she mumbled as his hand fell away to open the plate glass doors. And never was she more glad to feel the air outside on her face.

'Goodnight,' she called, regardless that it was still light, still afternoon, and received Nate's answering farewell as she reached her car and he walked on to his.

She was still trying to start the wretched thing when Nate in his gleaming Rolls purred by the back of her. She was still trying to coax some life into her Mini when his voice at her window observed, 'You appear to be having trouble.'

She smiled, because there wasn't much else she could do. Certainly not give way to frustrated tears that efficient though she might be inside the office, at anything mechanical she was hopeless.

'I'll have it checked over tomorrow,' she told him, still

fiddling with everything on the dash that looked promising but knowing in her heart of hearts she would be catching the bus home. She would have to send a mechanic to look at the perishing thing.

'Your battery's flat,' Nate diagnosed, amazing her with her lack of automobile knowledge that he hadn't even needed to lift the bonnet to come to his conclusion. 'Out you get—I'll give you a lift.'

'But you're in a hurry,' she reminded him.

'Did I say I was?' he answered, opening her door.

Kathryn found she was leaving her car, obeying his authority that he would give her a lift without thinking about it, her mind taken up with remembering he had said he wanted to leave early that night but had said nothing at all about being in a hurry.

No wonder Rolls-Royces purred, she thought, ensconced in his car—not having to tell him where she lived since he had already visited her on one occasion she was never likely to forget—she felt like purring herself from the pure luxury of it.

He drove the way he did everything, she couldn't help thinking as the car motored on, effortlessly and well. And while in the lift he had been disinclined to make conversation, while driving along he made several quite ordinary remarks that had her thinking that since technically this was still business time she was spending with him, perhaps he was extending burying that bone of contention between them until the hour struck five; for they had made no pact to be amicable with each other after that hour. Then she found to her disquiet that she was hoping he had got to know her a little better this week, as she had got to know him. She found she was actually hoping if ever they did meet after office hours—which she knew they wouldn't—that the way he had been with her at the office would continue!

Half way to her flat, he stopped to fill up with petrol. He remarked as he pulled off the forecourt, 'I should hate to run out of juice before I got to Surrey.'

'Surrey?' she enquired, and learned then that Nate didn't have a flat in London as she had supposed, but had the last time he had been home purchased a house on the outskirts of a village in Surrey and commuted to and fro daily.

'You knew you'd get the chairmanship?' she asked on impulse, regretting the impulse straight away, though she still did not see why he should buy a house in England if he thought he would be returning to America after that particular board meeting.

Nate was silent for some moments so that she thought he had objected to her question. Then she discovered she hadn't offended him, as he began to state the facts as he had seen them.

'With my uncle sounding me out on how Adrian would cope if the day ever came when it was left to him to run the American part of the business, it was a pretty safe bet that I had the present chairman's vote in my pocket.'

'Adrian wasn't offended his father didn't vote for him?' she enquired, enormously proud that Nate was opening up and telling her things he had no need to—well, not unless he had any wish to be friendly, she thought, feeling a glow that it wasn't just at the office he was being nice to her.

'Relieved, I should say,' Nate enlightened her. 'Adrian is married to a most delightful American young lady who's about to present him with their first child. He has no wish to uproot himself from America at the moment, or to take home work that will interfere with his enjoyment of his family.'

That sounded so lovely that for a moment Kathryn felt quite wistful that she didn't have a family-loving Kingersby to rush home from his work every night to her. That was until she recalled she could have had that had she married Rex. But Rex wasn't the Kingersby she wanted! Horrified at the direction her thoughts were taking, she jumped in with the question:

'What about your other cousins? Didn't any of them want the job?'

'Tim isn't ready for the responsibility yet,' Nate told her easily. 'Jeremy wouldn't have minded, though he voted for me too. And Paul,' she happened to turn and saw his face crease into what could only be called a grin and knew then that he had a lot of time for Paul, 'well, not to tell tales out of school, I rather think Paul is having too good a time in France to want to leave in a hurry.'

Smoothly the Rolls pulled up outside the house where Kathryn had her flat. The atmosphere in the car was as friendly as she would wish it, so that when the idea that had been nowhere in her head a moment ago, when recalling that Nate had to drive to Surrey, she found she was impulsively asking:

'Would you like to come in for a cup of tea before . . .' her voice faltered at the way he looked down his nose as if she had surprised him by her impudence, 'or—or perhaps you'd rather wait for your tea until you get home,' she tacked on lamely, wanting only to flee as pink colour rushed to her face.

Nate's hand stayed her when she turned from him to hunt frantically for the door catch. 'What a lovely girl you are, Kathryn,' he addressed her back. And when perforce she just had to turn round, she saw he was smiling. 'Forgive my reaction, but you constantly surprise me.'

'I do?' she exclaimed chokily, seeing he didn't look to be at all offended by her impudence now.

He nodded, doing nothing for her composure by raising a hand and gently running a couple of fingers down her crimson cheek. 'You've just surprised me again,' he told her, his mouth curving, that bottom lip taking a particularly sensuous look. 'There was I thinking I'd worked you so hard again this week that you'd refuse my offer of a lift because you'd had enough of me. But not only did you accept a lift, but here you are out of the goodness of your heart offering to refresh me before I drive on.'

His fingers left her cheek, but she felt her cheeks were still burning as she sought round for something that wouldn't give away the emotions that were having a riot of a time within her.

'Er—the offer's still open if you would care . . .' she tried.

'Thank you, but I think not,' Nate said softly. 'Your goodness is more than I deserve after the terrible time I gave you all last week.'

At that moment she had forgotten how completely dreadful last week had been. But some inner reserve wouldn't have her letting him think she was pushy by offering again.

'I'll—er—see you on Monday, then,' she said quietly, and turned, this time finding the door handle without any difficulty. She had half turned back ready to say goodbye, then just couldn't move at all. For Nate had moved closer, his head only inches from her, and she just knew with certainty that he intended to kiss her mouth, his eyes on her lips told her so.

'Thank you for not holding last week against me, sweet Kathryn,' he murmured, and as her eyes began to close as his face came nearer, she felt warm lips briefly caress her cheek.

Her eyes flew open to see he had moved back, was not intending to kiss her mouth at all. 'G-goodbye, Nate,' she said hurriedly, and went, holding on to as much decorum as she could while she thought he might be observing her, to race up to her flat once out of his sight, enormously

glad his mouth hadn't touched hers. For just the feel of his
kiss on the side of her face had started the most unimagin-
able longings inside her!

A half an hour later she was still sitting in the seat she
had dropped into when she had come in. She was still
wondering what on earth was happening to her. Was Nate
Kingersby some kind of sorcerer, that without effort he
seemed to have the power to bewitch her?

Take any day up until last Friday and she would have
walked home barefoot rather than accept a lift from him.
Not that he would have offered her a lift last week. Yet in
only a week of seeing this other side of him, when she knew
how foul he could be if the mood was on him, she had not
only invited him in for a cup of tea, but had been witless
when he had kissed her cheek, had been lost for a moment
then in wanting—to be in his arms!

There wasn't any sense to it, she thought, getting up and
trying to come to terms with the havoc Nate created within
her. Why, if things had happened as they should have
happened, she would right at this moment be married to
his brother, be his sister-in-law! Thank God she hadn't
married Rex, was all she could think about as she put the
kettle to boil.

She wasn't in love with Nate, she was sure she couldn't
be. But she definitely wasn't ready to marry anybody if a
man such as he could come along and without stirring
himself too much, send some of his charm her way, and have
feelings starting up inside that Rex had never had her
giving in to.

By the time she went to bed that night, Kathryn, with an
honesty she found mortifying, had to own that not only had
she had a narrow escape in not marrying Rex, but that if
his brother could have her emotions acting so erratically
with so little cause, then she had done Rex Kingersby something of a favour when she had given him back his ring.

The next morning, thinking the Kingersby family had occupied too much of her thoughts just lately, Kathryn set about breaking the habit. First she rang Fay Cooper, a friend who lived not far away but whom she had written to and told the wedding was off, and asked her if she had nothing else doing if she fancied a visit to the cinema.

'I've promised Debbie Hutton I'd go along to her party tonight,' Fay said, urging, 'Why don't you come too? You know Debbie and all that crowd.'

'I couldn't, not without an invitation.' Kathryn backed away from the idea of going to Debbie's party—wild wasn't the word for the way her parties ended up.

'She'd gatecrash one of yours without a second thought,' said Fay, and deciding for herself that Kathryn must be feeling low whoever was responsible for the broken engagement, wouldn't hear of her spending the evening alone. 'If it bothers you I'll give her a tinkle and ring you back,' she said, and rang off before Kathryn could ask her not to bother.

Why the crowd she had gone around with before she had got herself engaged to Rex should now appear juvenile in the antics they got up to, Kathryn hadn't a clue. But as she looked up the telephone number of a garage near to where she worked, feeling lost without her car, she tried to find some enthusiasm from somewhere for the party.

It was what she needed, wasn't it, she argued mentally against the pull to find a good book and stay in with her feet curled up. She needed to get back into circulation again, to get the Kingersbys out of her mind. To discover again that her life didn't revolve around that family.

She got through to the garage, told them about her flat battery and where they could find her car. And since apparently they envisaged having no trouble in finding a key to fit her Mini, for they seemed not to require her car keys to get inside, said she could ring them in an hour to see if Nate's flat battery diagnosis had been accurate.

There were always chores to do on Saturday morning, and what with Fay Cooper ringing back to tell her to let the moths out of her glad-rags, that Debbie would be mortally offended if she didn't show, the next hour passed quickly.

Kathryn collected her car late in the afternoon and tried to look as if she knew what the stand-in service manager was talking about when he told her she had a faulty dynamo.

'Have you repaired it?' she asked, not knowing whether a faulty dynamo had to be repaired or replaced, but thinking the trouble must have somehow been corrected since she had been told on the phone when she had rung back that she could collect her car around four.

'We only have a skeleton staff at weekends,' she was informed. 'You'll have to book her in if you want us to do a proper job on it. We've recharged your battery, so it will go on for some time yet.'

'It's not urgent that I have the—er—dynamo fixed straight away, then?'

'Well, it'll have to be done some time,' said the man whose presence seemed to be needed in half a dozen places at once as a young liberally-covered-in-grease mechanic hovered a yard away and the phone in the tiny office started to ring.

Kathryn backed out of the office as he went to answer the phone, thought fleetingly of having a word with the mechanic, then changed her mind as he gave a long-suffering sigh that the service manager had answered the phone when he could see he was waiting to speak to him.

Her Mini started first time, and as Kathryn drove happily away from the garage, she mused that with her car to her untrained ear sounding perfect, and since the garage man had given her the impression that any vague future date would do to have her dynamo done, then it could wait until the next time it started to misbehave itself.

Knowing the party wouldn't be under way before eight-thirty, at nine that evening having every intention of driving herself home, she arrived at the party still trying to convince herself how much she was looking forward to it when Debbie answered the door to her knock.

'So pleased you could make it, Kathryn,' she welcomed her warmly. 'Go on through. You know everybody, I think.'

Fay straight away roped her into the group she was with, and a drink of something that smelt lethal was soon pushed into her hand. And for all everybody was laughing and joking, and talking so hard it was difficult to get a word in on occasions, in less than thirty minutes Kathryn was wondering what she was doing there.

For the look of the thing she spent the following hour in dancing, chatting, warding off unwanted advances, and generally trying to look as though she was having a great time. But her heart wasn't in it. And at eleven, finding her hostess alone for two seconds, she quickly made her excuses and was the first to leave, knowing she had outgrown this particular type of party.

On Sunday she reflected that in preparing herself for the responsibilities of marriage, short though her engagement had been, in those few months her outlook on life had matured somewhat. The party last night had proved that.

Not that she regretted having once been one of that noisy, anything-for-a-laugh crowd; it had all been a part of growing up. But as she pressed a suit ready for work the next day and recalled the lack of enthusiasm with which she had got ready last night, it came home to her that she was looking forward to working with Nate tomorrow with far more eagerness than she had looked forward to going to the party.

Perhaps I'm a career girl at heart, she thought the next morning when she parked her car, her eyes going in the direction of where Nate usually parked his and seeing he had arrived. She certainly found her new boss gave fresh vitality to the work she did at any rate.

'Good morning,' she called when she went in, unconsciously humming to herself as she popped down her bag with one hand and lifted the typewriter cover off with the other.

'You sound happy this morning,' said Nate, coming through from his office.

Her eyes flicked to him and away, noting in that quick glance that he had a darker grey suit on this morning and how well it became him. Her insides went weak as in a flash the memory of how she had felt when he had lightly kissed her on Friday came back, and she hoped with all she had that her face wasn't looking as pink as it felt.

'I am,' she said, and wished she hadn't. For glancing at him again she saw he was frowning, and thought then he might be thinking it unpardonable that she should be so on top of the world when through her his brother had driven when incapable of driving.

She felt better when his frown disappeared, for all his, 'Must have been a good film,' mystified her until she recalled she had told him she might go to the cinema over the weekend.

'Oh, I didn't go to the pictures,' she said, ridiculously happy to see he was favouring her with that curving half smile. 'I went to a party.'

'Who with?' he bit out aggressively, his look changing darkly, causing her spirits to dip that he still didn't believe she hadn' ditched Rex for some other man.

And it annoyed her too that in the space of a very few minutes he could have her emotions going up and down like a yo-yo. 'Nobody you know,' she snapped—then felt sick with herself that she could snap at him when he must still be worried about his brother, and dared to ask, anger gone, 'Is Rex all right? I mean . . .'

'You care?' he barked, and strode back to his office.

For a week that had started off so very badly, by the time Friday came round again Kathryn was beginning to think it was one of the best weeks she had ever spent. They had worked hard, Nate hadn't let up at all. But where on Monday morning she had thought she would be glad to see Friday, she had come back from her lunch to see a single yellow rose stuck in a tumbler of water on her desk. And although Nate had not apologised for being so rough on her, she accepted his rose as his apology and from then on things had gone swimmingly.

And if occasionally she caught him giving her what looked like a hard-eyed stare, she knew it wasn't really. For apart from the light playing tricks at the distance between the two offices, she now knew he had a tendency to over-concentrate. He would look up from what he was doing, see her, but not see her at all, his mind filled with the business matter in hand.

They worked until after five on Friday, but staying a few minutes over never had bothered Kathryn.

'That's it, I think,' said Nate at last, passing over the letter he had just signed. And, his voice not unpleasant, 'Partying again this weekend?'

'No,' she said, and seeing he had mentioned the subject without looking as though he was going to blast her felt she could explain, without knowing why she should, 'That—er—party I went to last Saturday,' and feeling stupid that he was showing only polite interest, 'it was an impromptu sort of thing. I—left early.' She saw his eyes narrow and following the construction he must have put on that, she rushed in to forestall any thunder, 'By myself, I mean. I drove myself home.' Then she could have hit him for the fool she felt she'd made of herself, when all he said was a cool:

'Car going all right now, is it?'

'Yes,' she said, leaving it at that. To explain to him what was still as clear as mud to her about her dynamo would only have her feeling an even bigger fool if he asked some question that was remotely technical.

On Saturday morning she was in the middle of her chores when Fay Cooper rang up for a chat, going on about Debbie's party and asking where had Kathryn got to, before she got round to suggesting the cinema that evening.

'Love to,' said Kathryn, and went back to her chores thinking perhaps she would invite Fay back to supper afterwards.

To this end she went out shopping for a few supplies during the afternoon. She had only just got back and was putting away the things she had bought, when there was a knock on her door.

As she had not expected to see Nate Kingersby until Monday, her surprise to see her tall good-looking boss standing there had no need to be disguised. What she did disguise, or tried to as a smile left her, was the pleasure that rushed through her to see him there.

'Come in,' she said after a moment of being lost for words.

Closing the door as he entered her sitting room, she saw his eyes were observing that there were several homely touches about the place now, where the mantel-piece had been devoid of ornament, bookshelves empty of books the last time he had been here.

She had no idea why he had called, and was on the point of wondering if he had time to stay for a cup of tea, when the dreadful thought struck her that perhaps Rex had had a relapse and that Nate had called to plead with her to go to him.

But even while these thoughts were chasing through her mind, Nate turned his head, and from that slow half smile that showed for her she was sure his visit had nothing to do with his brother.

'I hope you don't mind me calling like this,' he said, 'but I was in the area, so I thought since I have a favour to ask I would come personally rather than phone.'

'Favour?' she asked, wondering if her portable typewriter would be up to it if he wanted her to do some work, for all he hadn't his briefcase with him. Belatedly she thought to invite him to take a seat.

That half smile was there again as he waited with inbred courtesy for her to be seated before he complied. 'I find myself in something of a dilemma,' he explained, looking big, relaxed and at home in one of her chairs. 'Last week I accepted an invitation to join a friend's dinner party tonight. This morning I rang my host to enquire if his wife had any preference for any type of flowers I intended having sent to her . . .' He broke off as though embarrassed suddenly.

Amazed that the man of the world she was sure he was should ever entertain an emotion such as embarrassment, Kathryn tried to help him out.

'You want me to send the flowers for you?' she questioned, knowing other secretaries sometimes did that sort of thing, though not really seeing why such a request had necessitated him calling to see her in person.

'No,' he said, a shade shortly she thought, as if impatient with her obtuseness. Then he smiled, and she forgave him, seeing his impatience was brought about by his embarrassment when he explained, 'It hadn't occurred to me, until Leigh mentioned it this morning, that I shall upset a well thought out table plan if I turn up without a partner.' That he was not at ease in what he had to ask her was evident in the way he rubbed the bridge of his nose before he went on. 'In the short time I've been back in England my spare time has been filled in working on a five-year plan for the company and also . . .'

He didn't finish; he didn't need to. Kathryn had no need to be told of the many hours he had put in at Rex's bedside. But still she was no further forward in seeing, if he didn't want her to send his hostess flowers, what then the favour was he had come in person to ask.

'What I'm trying to tell you, Kathryn,' he said, without knowing it giving her the firm impression he thought two short planks had nothing on her for thickness, 'is that not having had time to play since I've been back, I'm not yet into having a little black book filled with females I can contact at short notice.'

The small feeling of indignation that had started to surface, that he didn't think much to her brightness in his dilemma, faded quickly as excitement at what he might be meaning leapt in her heart. Women, she didn't doubt, fell down for him like ninepins, but what he was asking, she thought with growing conviction, bearing in mind how well they had got on with each other these last two weeks, was that in a purely platonic way, would she agree to be his dinner partner. She saw then the reason for his embarrassment. No man with his sort of virility would like to confess that his little black book was full of blank pages.

'W-would you like me to partner you?' she asked nervously. Had she got it wrong? Perhaps he had no intention of letting the harmony they had shared this past two weeks extend beyond five o'clock? But this was Saturday—she checked her nerves. Nate was here now, being pleasant, and Saturday wasn't a working day.

'I was hoping you would volunteer,' he said, his relief obvious. 'Though I would have understood, of course,' and his voice became teasing, 'had you decided a visit to the cinema was a better proposition.'

'Oh, help!' Kathryn exclaimed. 'I've made arrangements for tonight.' She saw that dark frown that had been in evidence on Monday, and knew then that he wasn't going to believe she had an arrangement to go out with a girl friend.

'I see I've wasted my time,' he said shortly, and stood up.

'No, you haven't,' she said quickly, seeing straight away that if she couldn't convince him he would not only hate her for allowing him to tell her all he had, but also for still going about with the man he thought she had decided was a better proposition than his brother. 'We girls have a code developed from our campfire days,' she said. 'If you don't mind waiting I'll ring Fay, the girl I was going to see a film with, and remind her of the unwritten law made over burnt sausages.'

She knew she was chattering nonsensically away purely because she was going to feel awful if Nate strode through that door. He had teased her, she thought as she dialled Fay's number, hoping she was in, so maybe he would think that had given her licence to tease him in return.

'Hello, Fay,' she said, glad to hear her, and saw Nate was already at the door, but had halted. Then she concentrated on getting out of her prior arrangement for that evening. 'Do you mind very much if we go to see that film another night?' she asked, hoping her friend wasn't going to be sticky.

'Something better come up?'

Kathryn looked at Nate coming slowly back into the room. She smiled down the phone. 'Yes,' she said.

'Lucky you! If he has a pal remember me.'

'Thanks, Fay,' she said, and put down the phone. And so happy was she suddenly that she was having a job keeping her face straight. She looked at Nate and asked, a gurgle of laughter in her, 'Would you have a girl miss Robert Redford *and* her dinner?'

Laughter stayed with her when unbelievably she saw whatever charm she had of her own had got through to

Nate. For once again she saw that smile in him that appeared
to be more genuine than any others, saw that smile suddenly
change into a definite grin.

'Would I let a girl starve!' he answered.

CHAPTER SIX

WHY she should so be looking forward to the evening she was to be spending with Nate, Kathryn could not have said. What she did know was that if she wasn't to keep him waiting when he called for her at seven—ample time, she had thought at the time, to get ready—then she had better take a few minutes out to calm herself, then get a move on.

It was ridiculous to feel like this—like some teenager going off on her first date. As far as Nate was concerned she was just doing him a favour by partnering him. He would be amazed if he knew how the prospect of going out with him had unsettled her. Amazed too if he ever had any idea of what his kiss on her cheek that time had done to her.

Good heavens—she calmed the sudden hurried beat of her heart as that kiss was remembered—there would be nothing like that tonight. That kiss had been in the nature of an apology for the brute he had been to her. He wouldn't be kissing her again. Their outing was platonic, nothing more.

At five to seven she was ready, dressed in a flame-coloured jersey dress that had been part of her trousseau. Kathryn knew she was looking good and was glad—though she had some severe worrying moments when she wondered that she didn't feel any pain at donning the dress she had purchased to look good in for Rex. She felt instead only gladness that she had something in her wardrobe that wouldn't make Nate ashamed to introduce her to his friends.

Her feeling of pent-up excitement took a sharp drop when the most horrifying thought came. Had she inherited some of her father's fickleness, that having thought herself to be in love with one man, she could so soon have no room for him in her mind, all her thoughts centred on the man who would be calling for her any moment now?

She sat down to wait, trying to oust that dreadful suspicion. Would it have waited until she was twenty-four to show itself? she fretted, loathing as she did the fickleness of her father's nature.

She got up to begin pacing the room, trying to come to terms with the fact that if there was one characteristic she admired more than any other it was fidelity of nature, yet in an agony of wondering if that one characteristic that was showing this late in the day was one she hadn't got.

Oh no, it couldn't be, she agonised—and found salvation from the torment of her thoughts that why then so soon after Rex had she been so feverishly waiting for Nate to call. For at that moment a knock sounded on her door, and all emotions save the excitement on seeing him again were aroused, vanished as she knew he had come.

'Hello,' she said, inviting him in, blood rushing to her head, her heart wild within her to see how superb he 'ooked in his dinner jacket.

Nate Kingersby crossed her threshold and closed the door, his eyes never once leaving her. Kathryn watched, a roaring in her ears as his eyes travelled over the length of her, lighting on her breasts, the curves of her hips, and back to her face, her shining eyes revealing how pleased she was to see him.

'Your mirror will have told you you look absolutely stunning,' he said, no smile about him, his voice level as he stood looking at her, his eyes going from her shining dark hair to her eyes, to her mouth. 'Any words of mine would be superfluous.'

'W-would you care for a drink?' Kathryn offered, her heart still uncontrolled as the knowledge that had just come to her threatened to fracture all semblance of composure.

'I could do with one,' said Nate, causing her to think from the way he was still looking at her that the sight of her out of a business suit or the jeans she had been wearing that afternoon left him needing something steadying. 'But I think I'll leave it until we get to Blanche and Leigh's.'

'I'll get my coat,' she said, turning swiftly, needing to have hours alone by herself to come to terms with the astonishing truth that had revealed itself the moment she had set eyes on him again, seconds only available to her.

Whether Nate thought it odd or not she just had to close the bedroom door, close it and lean against it. Oh, my God, she thought, the reason for all the high excitement all too startling clear. She was head over heels in love with Nate Kingersby!

The knowledge knocked her sideways, had her mouth going dry as foolishly she tried to deny it. But she had to look what was in front of her straight in the face, and was shaken again that no matter how much she didn't want it to be true, it was there still.

She was in love with Nate—real love this time, not that girlish emotion she had felt for Rex. Not that emotion, tepid she now saw, that even while thinking it strong enough to want to marry him she had never been able to give herself to him as Rex had wanted. She had thought then that the reason had been that her inner self had known it wasn't right before they were married. But she saw blindingly now that it wasn't prudery that had kept her from Rex's bed, had him finding another woman to fill that need, but was because deep, deep down that strong sense of fidelity had told her she wasn't truly in love with him.

With Nate, her love was true. She saw that clearly. She saw the reason now for the emotions that had rioted within her when all he had done was kiss her cheek. She loved him with a love that knew no holding back.

Belatedly realising he would be wondering what she was

doing all this time, Kathryn picked up her coat from where she had placed it on the bed. She took one deeply swallowed breath and went towards the door, a smile she couldn't hold back breaking as she opened it and realised at just that moment that she had not after all inherited any of her father's fickleness. A deep and abiding love was the reason for her excitement where Nate was concerned—it had nothing at all to do with fickleness. For glancing at him she just knew without having to question how she knew, that the love she had for Nate Kingersby was a love that would endure for the rest of her life.

She tried to control the shiver of delight that touched every inch of her as taking her coat from her he placed it, his hands impersonal, over her shoulders.

'Ready?' he queried, nothing about him now appearing in the need of an alcoholic steadier as he gave her that half smile.

'Ready,' she agreed, and would have been perfectly happy to sit without saying a word as he drove to his friends' home, had not Nate made occasional conversation which, if she didn't want him to think that after five p.m. on any day she lost her tongue, meant she had to join in.

Leigh Atkins, tall like Nate, was about the same age, though where Nate had a thatch of thick dark hair, some of Leigh's crop was starting to recede. Kathryn liked him on sight, as too she took to his wife Blanche, a thin woman with a wide mouth that was no stranger to a smile as she hooked her arm through Kathryn's, saying she would show her where she could leave her coat.

In all there were a dozen people seated at dinner. And Kathryn was more glad than ever in the well-to-do company present, servants serving them with a delicious meal, that she felt equal to them all in her new dress.

She was in the middle of listening to what the man, introduced to her as Dudley Palmer, to the right of her was saying when she heard someone ask Nate how Rex was doing, and lost track completely of what Dudley was saying as she waited for Nate's reply.

'Maintaining progress, I'm glad to say . . .' she heard, the only report she had had since she had stopped ringing the hospital herself, afraid the staff would tell Rex she had telephoned and thereby give him false hope that they might get back together again.

'I'm sorry,' Dudley was obviously waiting for a reply to something he had said, 'I didn't hear the last bit.'

'I'll have to get Leigh to do something about the acoustics in here,' Dudley quipped. 'I was sounding you out, actually.'

'Sounding me out?' Kathryn queried.

'Trying to find out if that lucky dog Nate has a call on all your free time, and if not is there a chance you might come out with me?'

'Oh,' she said, stumped for a moment. 'Er—actually . . .' she began, not wanting to snub him, but the only man she ever wanted to go out with was sitting opposite her.

She looked at Nate then and saw he was unsmilingly watching her. She knew suddenly that he had heard what Dudley had said, then felt joy idiotically that for all he might well think she had been leading Dudley on, he turned his attention to him and remarked:

'Find your own girl-friend, Palmer—leave mine alone.'

Unable to look at either of them after that, Kathryn found the petits fours of the utmost interest. Dudley Palmer was partnered by his sister, seated next to Nate, and from the way she had been hanging on to his every word it didn't take any genius to work out that she would have given her right arm to have been the first entry in Nate's little black book. So Kathryn felt doubly pleased that for all his remark had meant nothing other than that he might have noticed she had been struggling to give Dudley a polite brush-off,

Vesta Palmer could not now be in any doubt that for this evening at any rate, Nate had his own girl-friend with him, and Vesta too was wasting her time.

After dinner a few people danced to the tape Leigh had put on. But her love was too new for Kathryn to know how she would cope if she found herself dancing, Nate's arms encircling her. She was quite content to stand with him, finding she was able to join in the conversation he was having with Leigh and another man. And the other man was not slow in sending her the occasional appreciative look.

Other people came up to them from time to time, and Leigh disappeared to circulate with his other guests. And it was some time later, Leigh having joined them once more as the hour neared midnight, and suggested another drink, that Nate refused, saying they were about to leave.

In the car on the way back to her flat there were several times when Kathryn wanted to thank Nate for the wonderful time she had had. But knowing the enjoyable evening had only turned into being wonderful because he had been there, she was too scared of giving herself away should she become effusive. And another moment passed when she could have said something when Nate, his voice sounding grim, said suddenly:

'Women like you should be kept under lock and key.'

'Why?' she asked, startled as much by the grimness of his tone as by what he had said.

'Don't tell me you didn't notice the way Chivers was looking ready to eat you. Not to mention the way that young sprat Palmer couldn't keep his eyes off you.'

Chivers must have been the man in their quartet straight after dinner, she thought, remembering vaguely Leigh making the introduction, but too full of anguish that Nate appeared to be thinking she had invited his glances to remember more. 'It wasn't my fault,' she said. 'I can't help it if . . .' She stopped, the most shattering thought coming to her. Was Nate—jealous?

'You hook men without even trying, don't you?' he said, staring straight in front of him, his attention on his steering, the dislike for her in his voice making a mockery of her stupid thought that he might be jealous.

The dashing of her hopes that she affected him in any way other than dislike for what she had done to his brother made pride surge so he shouldn't know how easily he could deflate her.

'Well, at least we know there's no danger of you ever being caught on my hook, don't we?' she said tartly.

Deeply hurt that the fool's paradise she had been in had shattered, she looked out of the side window. She had so enjoyed her evening, and had thought Nate had enjoyed it too. But the very way he hadn't bothered to answer showed that for all he seemed to think she could have any man dangling, it was obvious that whatever charms she was supposed to have had left him immune.

Then into the darkness of the car, so that she would have given anything to have seen his face, for all his words sounded sincere, he was rocking her suddenly by saying:

'I've spent all evening trying to deny how very much aware of you I am.'

Swallowing hard before she could speak, Kathryn managed to choke, 'You have?' and when he didn't answer found she loved him too much to leave it there. She just had to have a crumb to feed on. 'I—er—had the impression a few minutes ago that you didn't—er—like me very much.'

Nate negotiated a bend, drove on a little way to stop at some traffic lights, then as if he was aware she was looking at him, he turned his head. And then, very slowly, he smiled. And Kathryn smiled back, because he just wouldn't have smiled, would he—not if he hadn't liked her just a little bit.

All too soon he was halting his car outside her house.

Lightheaded just then, supremely happy that his smile must mean he had forgotten he had started out hating her and had begun to like her just a little, she turned ready with her thanks for the evening.

'I'll see you inside,' he said, opening the door his side.

Her heart started to race. Should she ask him in? They reached her landing, not saying anything, for Kathryn no words needing to be said. Outside her door Nate held his hand out for her key. Almost dreamlike she handed it to him, watching as he unlocked her door and pushed it inwards.

'W-Would you like you come in for coffee?' she asked quietly before he could wish her goodnight—and knew he wouldn't. She felt unmistakable disappointment just the same when he gave her back her key and took a step away, that half smile appearing as he looked down into her face.

'I think not,' he said, as she knew he would. Then, unbelievably, 'I find you much too heady by far, Kathryn.'

'What—do you mean?' she asked, unable to credit that he had just said what it had sounded like.

'I mean,' he spelled it out for her, and all at once his face was deadly serious, 'a man could all too easily lose his head over you—if he didn't watch himself.'

And before she could do more than gasp at what he had said, his hands had descended on her shoulders, he had pulled her close, seemed to be about to kiss her, then had pushed her sharply away and was going quickly down the stairs.

All the next day Kathryn couldn't get the last words Nate had spoken out of her mind. She had been on cloud nine as she went to bed and in no frame of mind to dissect them then.

But by the time she went to bed on Sunday night, the euphoria that had been with her twenty-four hours ago had vanished, and cold heartaching logic was in its place.

For it was all too obvious now that when Nate had indicated that *he* could easily lose his head over her, the rest of the sentence, 'if he didn't watch himself', could only mean that he had every intention of watching himself, of keeping his head.

Kathryn knew what lay at the bottom of it, of course. Knowing as she did how each one of the Kingersbys regarded each other, Tim Kingersby had definitely cut her one day last week, there was no way Nate was going to let that small liking he had for her grow into anything bigger. Not while he still considered that through her his brother had very nearly permanently crippled himself, the responsibility was at her door that Rex still had months of being in hospital in front of him.

Loving Nate as she did, she tried to think up ways in which she could tell him just why she had thrown Rex over. But each time, when visualising his face after she had told him everything, all she could see was dark hatred that she had dared to blacken his brother's character. Especially when Nate had told her already that Rex wouldn't tell him of their last meeting, believing as he did that Rex would die rather than blacken her name.

Her emotions were all over the place when she went to the office on Monday. She had told herself that not by word or deed would Nate have an inkling of how she felt for him. She was determined only to smile at him when the occasion really demanded it. She knew she would die a thousand deaths if he suspected from one unrestrained besotted smile how he made the world spin for her.

But the first thing she saw on opening the office door was a large vase full of red carnations. And she could do nothing about the smile that beamed from her as she looked from the flowers to Nate rising from his chair in the other room.

'I forgot to say thank you for filling in the breach at such very short notice on Saturday,' he said, coming towards her.

And taking her totally by surprise, he leaned forward and placed a whisper of a kiss on her forehead.

Then, not giving her time to reply, though speech had temporarily been taken from her, the imprint of his mouth burning on her forehead, he promptly returned to his office. And since his lightly given kiss had been a tribute of thanks, no more, Kathryn had to steady herself as best she could and try very hard to think like the business girl she had to be—at the office anyway.

Tuesday followed Monday as being another perfect day. She and Nate got on so well professionally that she went home both nights wishing she could explain and have his understanding about Rex, so that maybe she could have a chance with him outside their business relationship.

Nate had told her that when a Kingersby fell in love other women ceased to exist. Oh, to have a love like that! To have Nate love her the way she loved him. But it wasn't to be, she knew that. She knew too that when her three months working for him were up, and her faith with George Kingersby kept, then whether he liked her or not Nate would expect her to vacate her secretarial chair.

Well, she would make him realise he would be letting go one of the best secretaries in London, she vowed, and went to work on Wednesday determined to let him see what a treasure he would be losing when he accepted her letter of resignation at the appropriate time.

'Good morning,' she said cheerfully when she went in, then she plunged straight into her work, not unhappy to see lunchtime arrive when she could uncoil her spring for an hour.

Nate was out when she came back, but that didn't stop her charging through her work. And when he did appear, after being at a meeting, Kathryn found she had nothing left to do that wouldn't keep until tomorrow.

'You've been busy,' he commented when she followed

him into his office and placed his neatly typed correspondence before him.

'Some days one has more energy than others,' she said,
flattered he had noticed, but not wanting him to think she
had put herself out more than usual.

'Ah,' he said, 'that's the reason for your output, is it? And
there was me thinking you had a date tonight and were
anxious not to stay on a minute after five.'

When had she ever been in a rush to leave on the dot,
apart from that day she'd had an S.O.S. from Sandra? she
thought, starting to grow indignant in spite of herself that
Nate thought her efforts had been entirely for her own ends.
Well, maybe they were, but not in the way he was thinking.

'As it happens,' she said, her indignation showing, 'I
don't happen to have a date tonight.'

'In that case,' he said, ignoring her indignation and pro-
ceeding to send it flying, 'perhaps you would do me the
honour of dining with me?'

'Dine with you?' she exclaimed, her heart acting up again
as it did so often, usually without him having to say anything that stunned her.

'It's not compulsory,' he said, as if reading from her
exclamation that she wouldn't consider the idea. 'I just
thought since you dropped everything to do me a favour
last Saturday I should like to take you to dinner . . .'

'I don't need to be taken out to dinner as a payment for
some favour I did you,' her pride had her butting in. A flat
feeling came that if that was his reason for asking her out,
then it took away all the joy she had felt that he wanted to
go out with her. 'Anyway,' she added, 'I enjoyed myself on
Saturday, so I consider you owe me nothing.'

'Hell,' muttered Nate, 'of all the stiffnecked females . . .'
Woodenly she looked at him, watched as his eyes narrowed
briefly, then that half smile she was familiar with came out.
'Please, Kathryn Randle,' he said, with such charm her

pride sank without trace, 'will you dine with me tonight, for no other reason than that I think we both might enjoy it.'

'With pleasure,' she said, and had to laugh simply because he did at her prompt, pert answer.

Perhaps it's as well I don't go out with him all that often, she thought, churned up again as she bathed and dressed getting ready. I'm sure I'd be a nervous wreck if he was my steady date. Tears stung her eyes as she dwelt on how wonderful it would be if she went out regularly with Nate. And she lost herself in dreams of what would never be for the next ten minutes, so that in the end she had to scurry around to be ready in time.

Had Nate taken her to a Wimpy bar she would have been as happy; just being with him was enough. But it was to a hotel noted for the high quality of its cuisine that he took her. He was at his most charming as he guided her over the choice of her meal. And he appeared to be just as pleased to be with her as she was with him, so that she could only hope and pray he wasn't 'watching himself' tonight—that for tonight, impossible to imagine it as she found, he wouldn't care even if he did lose his head over her.

And as the evening progressed, the steak he had ordered delicious, served in a wine sauce, and with Nate proving himself a witty as well as a stimulating companion, Kathryn just sparkled.

Because of the work they shared, the office came in for discussion, but not for long. For Nate seemed to want to concentrate all his attention on the evening. On her, dared she hope!

'Your beautiful brown eyes make me want to forget work,' he said, a moment after she had enquired how things were going with the five-year plan he had mentioned he was working on.

Kathryn sparkled some more, her velvety eyes shining with pleasure. Hope reached a pinnacle in her desire for him to forget everything, not just work. She didn't want him remembering he had a brother, didn't want him to remember that because of Rex he couldn't allow any emotion she aroused in him to rule him.

All through the evening she had avoided mentioning his brother's name—and she had no intention of bringing him up now, when suddenly Nate said, 'Tell me about yourself, Kathryn, your life before I met you,' for all Rex had been part of her life before Nate had stormed into it.

She settled for telling him a little of her family background, though she would have been much more interested in hearing about his formative years. But dared not say so, because she was afraid that any reference he made to his growing up must have Rex coming into it somewhere, and without having to think about it she knew that once Rex's name was mentioned Nate would be remembering what she had done to his brother, and the evening that was going so well would be ruined.

'Well, you know I have a sister Sandra,' she began. 'Sandra is seven years older than me.' She stopped as his eyes glinted and rushed on, cursing herself for her stupidity. Seven years was the same age difference between him and Rex. She had reminded him of his brother after all! 'We were brought up by our parents in a village near Oxford,' she said hurriedly, and felt relief rush in when Nate gave her that half smile and encouraged:

'You still have your parents?'

'My father is still alive,' she said, and as she remembered him a coldness gripped her. Her father had only ever tolerated her and Sandra. All the love in their childhood had come from their mother. 'He—he married again shortly after my mother died,' she told him, no warmth in her voice now as she remembered the way he had been led sobbing from the graveside. 'Three months afterwards, to be exact.'

'You sound as though you don't approve,' Nate commented mildly. 'Are you aggrieved that he so soon tried to find happiness with another woman?' And when she didn't answer, 'He probably loved your mother so well that the only way he could find consolation in losing her was to turn to someone else.'

Kathryn didn't want this conversation. It was putting a damper on the evening. But she couldn't have her mother's memory tarnished by agreeing, and therefore lying, that her father had been distracted at her passing.

'He never loved anyone but himself,' she said, looking away from Nate, painful memories resurrected. 'I was on my way back from holiday when she died, though she hadn't been ill when I went away. He loved her so much,' she said, unable to avoid the bitterness in her from spilling out, 'that even ill as she was, his prowling instinct was too much for him, and he left her to go away for a few days with one of his women. His affairs were legion.'

For long moments, as she tried to get rid of her wounded thoughts, tried to recapture the happiness that had been in her before she had got started on the subject of her thoroughly selfish father, neither of them spoke. Then quietly Nate said:

'So that's the reason you have such a colossal aversion to infidelity. Fidelity means everything to you, doesn't it?'

'I'm not paranoid about it,' she said lightly, and would have smiled then as with a superhuman effort she stamped down on the past.

Only her smile didn't get started, for just then a terrible harshness came to Nate's face and he was suddenly biting through clenched teeth:

'Is that why you jilted my brother?' And not giving her time to answer, 'Because you carry a resentment against all men? Because you wanted to make some man pay for the pain your mother suffered during her married life?'

'No!' The exclamation shot from her in astonishment at the way he had analysed what she had told him. And with her breath catching in her throat she saw that he had changed completely from being the courteous host he had been. He wouldn't even allow her to finish when more slowly she tried, 'That wasn't the reason I . . .'

'No?' His harsh expression was cynically disbelieving. 'Why then *did* you jilt him? You knew damn well if it was fidelity you were after you had no need to look farther than Rex.' He'd got it all so wrong. But he wouldn't let her interrupt to tell him so. 'You timed it perfectly, didn't you?' he accused, nothing of the charming dinner companion about him now as he lashed her. 'Your misguided attempt to avenge your mother's sufferings on one of the male sex couldn't have been timed better, could it? What better way to humiliate him than by throwing him over a week before the wedding?'

'Nate, please!' she cried.

She saw then such a look of hatred on his face for her that she felt shocked, beaten, and knew then that any explanation she made would be seen as an effort to besmirch the Kingersby honour held dear by all of them. And loving Nate even while knowing all he felt for her at that moment was hate, her love went beyond her own personal need and she just couldn't hurt him—even if he didn't believe her should she try to tell him his brother wasn't the saint he thought him.

Striving for calm, she tried reason instead, needing to see something in his face other than hate. 'Had I wanted to humiliate Rex as you seem to think,' she said quietly, 'do you think I would have bothered to personally return his ring? Isn't it far more likely, if what you believe is true, that I'm—unhinged—because of my father's libertine ways, that I would have said nothing, but just left Rex standing there at the altar?'

Long agonising moments passed with Nate making no reply. And it was then Kathryn knew that the evening that had started out so beautifully was over. She reached for her bag, moved as though about to rise, then heard Nate's voice, quiet too.

'Why did you break off your engagement?'

She looked at him and her heart shed some of its sadness to see the hate had gone from him, his expression serious, his look direct.

'Do we have to discuss it, Nate?' And from her heart, 'Can't we just forget it?' She knew from the way his jaw jutted that she was asking too much. But the evening was already in ruins; she didn't think she could take seeing that hate return if she dared to tell him the truth.

Then amazingly, to her delight, Nate changed again, all enmity gone. He even gave her that half smile as he remarked, 'We do tend to end up fighting whenever the subject of my brother comes up, don't we?' Then with his smile disappearing, though not the cordiality of his expression, he asked, 'Tell me one thing, though, Kathryn——' She waited, ready to tell him anything since for the sake of retrieving the evening he seemed ready to put the subject behind him. 'Were you ever in . . . Do you still love him?'

There was only one man she loved. She looked at that man, 'I'm no longer in love with Rex,' she said softly.

It seemed a miracle to her that after that, by sheer personality, Nate soon had her laughing again. And if the memory of that scene half way through her dinner was something unlikely ever to be forgotten, then she was ready to pretend it had never happened, as once more Nate became a charming and attentive escort.

She had no idea of the time when he took her home, and didn't care. All she knew was that like last Saturday she didn't want the evening to end. But this time when he went with her to her door, took the key from her and opened the door, she held back the urge to invite him in for coffee—then found to her utter bliss that men like Nate Kingersby didn't wait for invitations if it was in their minds to prolong the evening.

With a warm look on his face he handed her back her key. 'Am I allowed to come in to apologise fully for upsetting you earlier?' he asked softly, and didn't need to wait for her reply as he followed her in, closed the door quietly, then reached for her.

Unhesitatingly Kathryn went into his arms, feeling a thrill of delight as those strong arms enfolded her. 'I'm sorry too,' she said huskily, looking up at him her heart in her eyes.

'Dear Kathryn,' he breathed, and then his mouth was coming down over hers.

An exquisite sensation shot through her whole being to feel those firm yet mobile lips on hers. Her own lips parted as unreservedly she kissed him back, thrilled as his arms tightened about her as he felt her response. And while still kissing her Nate had done away with her coat and was caressing her bare arms, kissing the hollows in her throat, making her moan with pleasure as he trailed kisses to her ears. He had her clinging to him, wanting to get closer, had her hands beneath his jacket, the feel of his body heat through his shirt adding to her heightened senses.

'Oh, Nate!' she moaned in ecstasy as his hands at the base of her spine pressed her against his lean hardness.

'Kathryn,' he breathed back, then claimed her mouth with his again, words unnecessary as his hands moved from her spine upwards, pressing her to him, crushing her breasts against him moments before his hands came to soothe away any slight pain his crushing might have inflicted.

The feel of his hands on her breasts over the top of her dress had her wanting to shed her clothes so she could feel his hands on her skin, her body his, no thought in her head of holding back. She loved him, wanted to be a part of him.

Only some inner shyness, some unwanted reserve saved her from undoing her zip herself, her need to show him she was his and wanted it to be so uppermost, as wild emotions sent all rational thoughts fleeing.

But it was at that moment that his hands on her body stilled. That moment that his arms about her slackened, and his mouth left hers.

Bewildered, for this was new territory for her, Kathryn had only instinct to guide her as to what happened now—for all every instinct in her was saying they should be moving to a more intimate, even closer embrace, not letting daylight come between their two bodies the way Nate was allowing, she knew herself lost.

She looked up into his face, still wearing that warm look for her, then into his eyes. And she knew then from the detached light coming to those blue eyes that Nate wasn't going to allow their lovemaking to go any further.

'Don't look like that, Kathryn,' he said, and she could have sworn there was mockery there as he added, 'as though someone has stolen your favourite toy.'

She could still feel the heat of his body, and swiftly dropped her arms, needing to grasp at whatever sanity she had left.

'You apologise so—so overwhelmingly, Nate,' she managed to drag from she knew not where, 'I couldn't help showing you how fully I forgive you.' She had to give a choky cough before she could continue. 'But you're right, of course. We both have a hard day at the office tomorrow. And—and you have that drive back to Surrey in front of you, haven't you?'

She stepped out of his loose hold. She knew her colour was high and wanted only for him to be gone. For while he was still here she had the most wanton longing to be back in his arms. Even so, she struggled and found exactly the right light note to enquire:

'Would you like coffee before you go?' and just had to hope he would refuse.

He did. But she felt glad she had asked when she saw the admiration in his eyes, reluctant though it appeared to be at the way she was handling this turn of events.

'I think not,' he declined. 'As you say, I have to drive to Surrey.'

She went to the door with him, still trying to appear as though her emotions had not received the biggest shake-up in her life, as though she was back on an even keel, which was very far from the truth.

'Thank you for a lovely evening, Nate,' she said, adopting a friendly attitude, for surely that was the way sophisticated people acted in this situation, and hoping that only she knew he had only to take her in his arms again for that passion, new to her, to flare out of control again.

'Thank *you*, Kathryn,' he said, his mouth curving in a smile. And it didn't seem at all strange when minutes before he hadn't looked at all as though he would be sleeping anywhere but in her bed, he took hold of her hand, raised it to his lips, gently kissed the back of it, and said before going smartly down the stairs, 'I'll see you tomorrow.'

CHAPTER SEVEN

ANY ideas Kathryn had had on working flat out to show Nate what a brilliant secretary he would be losing, had been done away with when she awakened the next morning. She had spent a considerable amount of time in thought after he had gone last night and was still of the same opinion she had come to then. It would be better all round if she left when her three months was up.

Though how she was ever to face him again after the wanton way she had been his for the taking, she didn't know, for all their parting had been amicable.

It made her curl up inside to recall the way she had wrapped her arms around him, the way she had pressed her body up against his, for all it had been Nate who had started it. She had an inner conviction that he would have ceased making love to her long before he had, had she made the smallest protest. But she hadn't protested. She had clung to him with nothing in her response to indicate the virgin she was. Who could blame him if he thought he would be just one of a string of lovers? From Rex's remarks to him he was already certain his brother had been her lover.

And remembering Rex, Kathryn had the answer to why Nate had called a halt to their lovemaking. He too must have remembered his brother. She could think of nothing more guaranteed to kill his ardour than to realise that the girl he held in his arms was the girl his loved brother had very nearly killed himself over.

She sighed as she bathed and got ready to go to the office. Rex would always be there to kill any relationship between

113

her and Nate before it got started. She might as well give up dreaming now that one day Nate might come to care for her. Nate just would not let that happen.

For the first time in the weeks she had been working for him, she arrived at the office before him. Crazy, frightening thoughts of—had he had an accident?—panicked her for the five minutes, for he had always been in first and done an hour's work before she got in. But when five minutes later he breezed in, she was so relieved she forgot about the nerves that had beset her about how was she ever to face him again, and actually found she was grinning inanely when he remarked as he passed through:

'Don't tell anybody—I overslept.'

The innocent 'You should have gone to bed earlier' so very nearly left her that she blushed just as Nate turned back to pick up the post from her desk that hadn't yet been started on.

For a fleeting second a warm look showed in his eyes as he observed her blush, and her blush deepened as she realised he was thinking it was on account of the way they had been locked in each other's arms last night. That scorching memory in no way helped her colour to fade, and then she felt even more confused as Nate bent and placed a kiss on the end of her nose.

But as he straightened she saw that any warmth in his expression had left him. 'There's a time and a place for everything,' he remarked gruffly, and marched into his office.

Kathryn knew herself puzzled by his attitude. It almost seemed as though he felt affronted that he had so spontaneously dropped that light kiss on her nose, she thought, a frown puckering her brow.

But her confusion departed as reason came to tell her she had Rex Kingersby to thank that any spontaneous gesture Nate showed her that had nothing to do with business would always have him feeling disloyal to Rex at some part in the proceedings.

But she was not left to feel unhappy about it for very long. Nate hadn't got very far in reading his post before he was calling her through, saying:

'Come and give me a hand here, Kathryn.'

She was in and out of his office most of that day. And she happened to be there when a call came in from Sandra.

'Take it in here,' said Nate, not appearing unduly put out by the interruption to what they were doing.

Kathryn smiled her thanks, then turned her attention to what Sandra was saying, a much more cheerful Sandra this time than she had been the last time she had telephoned her at the office. She started off by saying she and Vic had had a real heart-to-heart talk last night, and that to her amazement she had learned that the reason he so often went off the rails was because he was jealous of the time she devoted to their two daughters.

'Jealous?' Kathryn couldn't help the exclamation, not ready to believe it, even if Sandra did sound convinced.

'I was staggered too,' Sandra went on happily. 'I know I do tend to fuss around them, but I never dreamt Vic thought I was shutting him out. I'm forever telling him I love him, even when he's been—a bit naughty.'

Kathryn could have wept for her gullibility. Had Sandra forgotten his track record? But since her sister was bubbling over in the belief that her husband would stray no longer now she had discovered the root cause for his appalling behaviour, she just couldn't knock her down by telling her she didn't believe it for a minute.

'So things are going to be different in future?' she queried.

'Yes,' Sandra said enthusiastically. 'That's why I'm ringing you. There's a baby-sitting circle locally, worked out on a points system where mothers sit in while other mothers have a night out. I haven't got it all sorted out yet, but with Vic saying he wants to take me out tomorrow night and with him thinking I always put the girls first, I said yes. But now . . .'

'But now you're short of a baby-sitter until you get things organised,' Kathryn put in, unable to remember the last time Sandra had left the girls to go out and enjoy herself. 'Of course I'll come,' she said, adding swiftly, 'I'll come after work tomorrow—don't bother cooking for me, I'll have a knife and fork lunch.'

Sandra was so happy she would have gone on chatting all day. But, aware of Nate's eyes on her, that she was using up his time as well as her own since they had been checking something together, Kathryn cut short her thanks by saying they would have a chat tomorrow.

'Sorry about that,' she apologised, ready to get back to where they had been before the call.

'Do you often baby-sit with your sister's children, as well as dash to hold her hand at the drop of a hat?' Nate enquired, not pretending he hadn't been listening.

'No,' she answered, about to say, but that's what families are for, but changing her mind. She didn't want him to be reminded of *his* family, of the close ties that bound them. 'And from the way Sandra was talking she won't be calling on me to hold her hand in future.'

'Husband turned over a new leaf, has he?'

Knowing what it would do to Sandra if he hadn't, Kathryn dearly wanted to believe he had. 'I hope so,' she said fervently, and left it at that.

Nate was out with business associates for most of Friday, so Kathryn saw little of him until he came in just after four. And that hour remaining until five was much too short. She took no pleasure in anticipating the coming weekend. The way the two whole days before she would see him again stretched endlessly in front of her served to endorse just how hard she had fallen for him.

He went straight to his desk, the expression on his face as he looked at that accumulation of paper work saying he'd be lucky to get through by midnight, she noted as she followed him in to acquaint him with the telephone messages she had taken in his absence. And it grieved her that because she had to drive to Reading, even if he did ask her to stay late to help him, she wouldn't be able to.

He didn't ask her to work overtime, but his expression was wry as he looked up from the additions to his work in the shape of what had arrived by second post and remarked:

'Who'd be a company chairman!'

'You love it,' Kathryn returned, having seen for herself the way he thrived on the work involved.

Nate leaned back in his chair surveying her through slightly narrowed eyes, taking in her shapeliness, her long length of leg in her neatly fitting charcoal grey trouser suit—and suddenly setting her heart madly pounding by drawling softly:

'It's brought me into closer contact with you, Kathryn,' just as though he loved that too about the job, and doing nothing for her erratically beating heart by adding equally slowly, deliberately, 'But what's the good of that if it leaves me little time to get to know you better?'

'Get to know me better?' she queried, her voice husky as a faint pink coloured her cheeks.

'I had been hoping to ask you to dine with me tomorrow evening,' he revealed, every word music in her ears. 'I have to visit Rex tonight.' It was the first time Rex's name had been mentioned between them without a hint of frost coming into the air, which had the music still playing for her. 'Which means I shall have to take this little lot home to add to the mountain of work already awaiting my attention in my study.'

'You intend working all over the weekend?' she asked, careful not to let the disappointment that had just come to her show. It was unbelievable that Nate had wanted to take her out again, and she started to hate that the work they both enjoyed should come between his stated wish to get to know her better.

'I must,' he said, and to her surprise, because she was sure he was too confident of his ability ever to defer to anyone, 'I want that five-year plan I told you about completed ready to show my uncle when he comes back.' And clearing up for her his reasons for wanting to consult George, 'He's still on the board, as you know, and I should hate him to think I'd come in and taken over without needing his advice.'

What a close knit-family they are, she thought, not for the first time—then knew herself concerned that Nate should work so hard. He had relaxed last Saturday at the Atkins' dinner party. He had taken her out on Wednesday— would she ever forget it?—but she didn't like at all to think that he would be slogging away all over the weekend without anyone there to help him.

'You'll make yourself ill,' she blurted out, her concern for him loosening her tongue.

'I don't know about that,' he answered, that half smile emerging, 'but I could certainly do with an extra pair of hands.'

'I could come and help.'

It was out before she could stop it. And aghast at what she had said—the last thing she wanted him to know was the extent of her caring, apart from the fact that she just knew he wouldn't want her within a mile of his home—she couldn't look at him. She expected any second to have him bluntly turning her offer down, but as the silence that had greeted her offer went agonisingly on, in the end she just had to look at him. Then she saw, incredulously, her heart going haywire, that Nate actually seemed to be considering her offer.

'We'd certainly get it done quicker with two of us at it,' he said slowly, sending her spirits soaring, then having that yo-yo effect on her again as he added, 'But I don't know, Kathryn.' And it had nothing at all to do with him not wanting her in his home, she saw, her heart starting to thunder, her spirits rocketing upwards when at last he said, 'From your point of view I don't know that it's such a good idea. You must have some idea of the way in which I regard you.'

'Er——' she began, struggling to see if what he meant was what she thought he meant. 'You—er—like me a little?' she suggested shyly, and saw he wasn't smiling at all as with his face almost stern he told her:

'I thought I'd shown you more clearly the effect you have on me.'

Kathryn feared heart failure at any moment, for as she remembered the way he had begun to make love to her on Wednesday, she thought, surely he could only be saying that he—more than liked her? He had said he wanted to get to know her better. Could she hope—and recalling too the way he had said a man could lose his head over her—dared she hope that he was saying he was starting to fall in love with her? Feeling dizzy from the hopes of her thoughts, she was afraid to ask, held back by that reserve that said any declaration of whatever his feelings for her were, that declaration must come voluntarily, uninvited, from him. But even so, she just couldn't risk not seeing him again for two whole days.

'Er—then why isn't it such a good idea that I come to do some work for you tomorrow?' she queried huskily.

His blue eyes studied her warm colour for several seconds before he answered. And then he was laying it on the line so that she shouldn't be under any misapprehension.

'Because, Kathryn my dear,' he said, his endearment thrilling her, 'I have an idea that even with two of us at it, the work I want to get through might well run into Sunday. And knowing the sweetness of you, I can't be sure I would refuse if you volunteered to stay with me until the work has been completed.'

Kathryn knew then what it meant when she'd read of women fighting for the men they wanted. 'Does it matter if I stay overnight?' she asked, and couldn't help that she crimsoned again. 'I mean—well, you said you intended asking me out on Saturday night. There's little difference, is there? I mean, the only difference will be that—if I do stay—er—overnight, you won't have a long drive after you've seen me home.'

'As I said, you're very sweet,' Nate said softly. 'But I must tell you, Kathryn, that as I've only just moved in, what with my new job and visiting Rex, not only is my home not yet completely furnished, but I haven't got round yet to finding myself a housekeeper.'

'You're saying we would be in the house—alone,' she choked, loving the idea, but hoping he was thinking it bothered her just a little. She didn't want him thinking her forward, for all her feelings for him were far from reserved.

'That's exactly what I am saying,' he told her. 'Though if you're worried I could promise you I have sufficient of the rooms furnished for you to have your own bedroom.'

Her cheeks burning, not seeing after last Wednesday how he could think she was some shy retiring female, but hoping he would think her high colour was because she had never doubted she would have her own room, Kathryn forced a smile.

'Well then,' she said, 'what's the problem?'

'None at all, by the look of it,' said Nate, and from the satisfied look on his face, she just knew he was as pleased as she was that it looked as though they were not going to have to wait until Monday to see each other again.

It was in a state of elation that instead of driving directly to Reading as she had planned, Kathryn sped hurriedly back to her flat after she left the office, exchanging her overnight bag for a weekend case, intending now to drive straight from Reading in the morning to Nate's home. For any thoughts Nate had had on the wisdom of her working with him at his home had been negated for no other reason than that it was what they both wanted. And he had not pretended otherwise, as straightaway he had gone into details of the exact location of his house.

Sandra was as bubbling over as she had been on the phone when Kathryn presented herself on her doorstep, looking more radiant than she had ever seen her.

'Vic's upstairs changing,' she said, taking her into the kitchen, ready to make her a cup of coffee. 'Oh, Kathryn, isn't it wonderful!'

And because she was experiencing for herself the thought that someone she loved so utterly might be loving her in return, Kathryn could do none other than agree.

She saw Victor briefly when Sandra, because it was so ingrained in her, couldn't resist going up to have a last look at the children.

'I mean it this time, Kathryn,' he told her before she could say a word, not doubting Sandra would have told her over the phone about their heart-to-heart.

'I hope you do,' she said solemnly, and couldn't keep back the heartfelt words, 'Don't hurt her again, Vic.'

'I won't,' he promised, and so looked as though he meant it that she obeyed the impulse and gave him a sisterly peck on his cheek.

She had a few minutes after they had gone to wonder if she had been too hard on her father. She remembered the love and devotion her mother had showered on her and Sandra, and for the first time began to see that her father might have been jealous of that devotion, the way Vic was of Sandra's devotion to Marigold and Gillie. And she had to wonder then if her father, in his own way, had loved her mother after all. She rejected the thought when she remembered the way he had left her alone when she had been ill, but she realised, when her thoughts swung from him and on to Nate, that she didn't feel as bitter about her father now as she had done. Had the love she had for Nate softened that bitterness?

Her anticipation of the time she was to spend with Nate, even though they would be working, had her singing softly to herself the next morning as she put her foot down to get to his home the sooner. Her heart flipped at the thought that maybe he might kiss her again, but that wasn't too important—not this weekend at any rate. More important was the fact that he had said he wanted to get to know her better. Well, she was all for that, though she tried not to hope for too much too soon, for all he had intimated his feelings for her were stronger than liking, hadn't he?

But as she drew up in front of the tall stately house that stood at the end of a long, long drive, her eager smile when she saw Nate come through the front door started to fade.

For as she got out of the car to greet him, she saw his face was far from welcoming, and only then did it dawn on her what an uphill battle she had on her hands. For clearly in between last night and this morning Nate had had second thoughts. Had seeing Rex last night endorsed for him that to allow himself to fall in love with her would be like stabbing his brother in the back?

'Hello, Nate,' she forced the cheerful greeting, not attempting to extract her case from the boot since it didn't look as though her overnight stay would be favourably looked on.

His greeting was so barely civil that had Kathryn not on that instant decided she would tell him exactly why she had broken with Rex, she would have got straight back into her car and left.

She went with him into the wide hall, her footsteps echoing back from the black and white stone chequered tiles, hoping when the time came for her to tell him that his feelings for her, whatever they were, would be too substantial for them to be turned into hatred.

But as she went into his study and saw from his crammed desk that he had already started work, and observed from his unsmiling look that he had no intention that the camaraderie they shared in the London office should spread into his home, she knew then that his hate was something she would have to risk.

But before they got down to work, Nate seemed to realise she had driven quite some way, though his face didn't lighten at all as he asked, 'Do you want some refreshment before you start?'

'No, thank you,' she said easily, her tongue hanging out for a cup of coffee. 'Sandra fed me such a huge breakfast I'm sure she thinks I'm wasting away.'

That brought his eyes flicking over her, but he merely grunted. And had she not seen that spark of admiration, infinitesimal and quickly extinguished as his eyes lighted on her, then she had a feeling she would have given up there and then.

But she had seen it, and as they got down to work, nothing in the sheer hard slog of the hours that followed would take away from her the fact that she had seen that spark.

Lunchtime came and went, and with Nate not noticing the time Kathryn could only hope he had breakfasted as well as she had. And she knew when three o'clock came and went, his cold attitude to her not letting up as he pressed on with what they were doing, that her weekend case would be staying in her car.

But it was at four o'clock, admitting she was flagging, that Kathryn's determination to ride out Nate's coldness to her began to weaken. How was she to ever get started on telling him about that awful scene she had witnessed in Rex's flat? she wondered. The way he had barked at her several times already had her knowing that if she so much as breathed his brother's name he would be marching her to her car before she could get another word out.

At a quarter past four mutiny entered her soul; his unfeeling attitude was getting on top of her. And instead of complying with his brusque order to re-check some percentage figure, she laid down her pen. Then very clearly, she said:

'I'm thirsty.'

That brought his head up to stare grimly, obviously soured that she had broken the rhythm of their work.

'Then go and get a drink,' he said sharply.

Kathryn stood up, tears near that all her hopes for that nebulous something to grow this weekend were now finally dashed.

'You've regretted asking—accepting my offer to come here, haven't you?' she said chokily, and saw a muscle move in his temple as he controlled some urge, probably to agree in no uncertain terms, she thought.

'A man has to do what a man has to do,' he quoted obscurely. And as tears started to her eyes, unable to bear that he was looking at her the way he had that first day they had met, as though he hated her, Kathryn bolted.

She never made it as far as the kitchen, although she headed in the direction where she thought the kitchen lay. Nor did she have time to get herself under control before she saw Nate again.

For silently he had come after her, had caught her in the hall, had taken her by the shoulders and was turning her round to face him. He looked down into her tear-drenched eyes, and as he swore softly he gathered her to him, pulling her head tightly into his shoulder.

'Oh, Nate,' she cried weakly, no longer feeling like weeping, her heartbreak gone now that those two strong arms were holding her.

But he shushed her quiet and continued to hold her in that comforting way. It gave her the strangest feeling that he was gaining some comfort too just from holding her. Though why he should be in need of any sort of comfort when he had been such a brute all day she couldn't fathom, and didn't try. It was enough to be in his arms where she felt she belonged.

And then with her need to tell him everything about Rex, the feeling came to her that she had his understanding now—he had understood without words that he was responsible for her tears, hadn't he?—she spoilt it all. She felt his arms slacken about her as she said:

'You've been horrible to me because of Rex, haven't you?'

His arms dropping away from her halted the truth she had been about to reveal. She saw his mouth firm into a tight line, saw his jaw jut, knew he had hardened his heart against her, just as she knew that her untimely reminder of his brother still injured and in hospital had made him wonder how he could have ever have forgotten he had once sworn in anger to get even with her.

And then while she watched—it was too shadowed in the hall for her to see if his eyes were smiling too—the firmness of his mouth began to curve into that half smile she knew so well.

'I've been a perfect swine to you today, haven't I?' he said to her amazement when she had been expecting to get blasted for so much as breathing his brother's name. And to her delight, he bent and lightly kissed her on the mouth, drawing back to add after a pause, 'You're right, of course. I have had Rex on my mind.'

And while her heart raced and she became convinced suddenly that he would listen without blowing his top to what she had to tell him, Nate went on to charm away any idea she had that she wanted to tell him anything about his brother.

'If I promise not to let thoughts of Rex intrude, not even to allow his name to come up between us, will you, Kathryn my dear, let me try to salvage what I was hoping in the office yesterday would prove a very happy time for both of us?'

She didn't have to think about it. 'Of course, Nate,' she said softly, and wanted to laugh joyously when he said:

'I'll start making amends by brewing that drink you're so desperate for.'

Since he drank two cups of tea when it was made, Kathryn could only gather that he was as thirsty as she was, as amicably they sat in the kitchen.

And her happiness was overflowing that when she thought he would now be ready to go back to work, he stood up, heading for the direction of the freezer standing in one corner, and muttered something about seeing what there was to eat for dinner.

'Dinner?' she exclaimed, beginning to feel hungry at the mere mention of the word. Then she saw Nate had turned and was smiling ruefully.

'Are you not going to allow me to show you I'm not loathesome *all* the time?'

Kathryn wasn't quite sure what he meant. 'You want me to stay to dinner?' she guessed.

'You weren't thinking of going back to London tonight, were you?' And while she was still trying to steady her heart, he came towards where she was sitting, and she was charmed again when he said, 'It won't take me a minute to make a bed up for you.'

She beamed at him simply because she couldn't help it,

and regardless of Women's Lib, told him, 'Making beds is a woman's work. I'll do it if you show me where everything is.'

The freezer forgotten, paper work forgotten, she went up the stairs with him, surveying the large bedroom with its enormous windows which he took her to and left her in while he went in search of sheets and blankets. They had passed other bedrooms on the way to this one. Open doors showed they were not furnished, as Nate had told her some of the rooms weren't as yet. Oh, how she would dearly love to go round the showrooms with him selecting pieces for his home, she thought. Not that he appeared to need her assistance, for this room with its creamy carpet and richly red-brown furniture, the double bed with its finial ends, showed he was not lacking in taste.

Nate came back, dumping the load he was carrying on to a lemon velvet covered chair, and Kathryn's happiness soared to new heights at the simple domesticity of it all when he went to one side of the bed and helped her to make it.

'Don't forget the hospital corners,' she grinned, and wanted to grab back the unthinking reminder she had given him of Rex when she saw his lips firm, his face hard before he bent to his task.

But that hard look had gone when he raised his head again, and once more he was the Nate who was doing all he could to make amends for the brute he had been, even looking pleased when she confessed she had her small case in the car. He sent her to get it when their bedmaking was completed, and left her at the bottom of the stairs saying he would go and find out what there was for them to eat.

Because, as it turned out, he was as hungry as she was, they dined early. And although what they ate was simple, chops and vegetables from the freezer, cheese and biscuits, to Kathryn's mind, because he had let her help prepare it, it was the best meal she had ever tasted. Their togetherness didn't come to an end when the meal was finished. For, insisting on doing the washing up, she found Nate had picked up a tea towel and was equally insistent on doing his share.

'I like this feeling of being partners,' he said, turning away as her eyes flew to him to place the plate he had just dried on the table behind them.

Afraid to speak, a glow suffusing her, she wanted him to know she liked it too. 'It is nice, isn't it,' she said quietly, finding the soap suds in the washing up bowl of the greatest interest.

He had no need to reply, and in fact didn't. But when she felt the thistledown kiss he planted on the nape of her neck before he reached for the next plate, Kathryn was glad her shaking hands were hidden in the sudsy water, keeping from him how much he disturbed her.

The washing up completed, and several hours yet of Nate's company before her until she went up to her room, she knew she had to make some attempt at normality if she didn't want him to guess her feelings for him. The time since he had caught hold of her in the hall and shown he wasn't averse to her company, and the very way he had not wanted her to go back to London that night seemed to confirm it. But she still had no clear idea of how he felt about her. And really, she thought, as she tried to keep a lid on the excitement that was threatening to spill over, she mustn't take the way he had said he liked their being partners as any sort of declaration.

'Hadn't we better get on with some work?' she said suddenly into the companionable silence that had settled between them. Work, after all, was the reason she was here.

Nate gave an exaggerated sigh that made her smile as he said, 'I suppose so. Though to tell you the truth, Kathryn, I would much prefer to sit here looking at you.'

Her heart somersaulted and her smile widened. 'That's no way to keep your job as company chairman,' she said as clearly as the constriction in her throat would allow, and had to swallow hard when Nate left his chair and came and placed an arm lightly round her shoulders, keeping his arm around her as he escorted her to where their work lay.

At half past nine he threw down his pen and declared that even company chairmen couldn't be expected to work such disgusting hours, showing his consideration was all for her when he added, 'It's not fair on you. You'd work until you dropped without complaining, wouldn't you?'

She couldn't tell him it hadn't seemed like work, that just to be with him, having the odd heartwarming remark thrown her way as they soldiered on, was all she needed to keep her from wilting. So instead she pretended she had had enough for that day.

'We can have a fresh start tomorrow,' she remarked as he led her into the sitting room, made sure she was comfortably seated, then went to fix her a drink.

He came back briefly to hand her the sherry she had asked for, then thrilled her anew when he raised his own glass to salute her, saying, 'To my lovely Kathryn.' And she was glad then that he turned to the tape deck, for she couldn't hope to hide that her eyes were shining from the possessive way he had called her his lovely Kathryn.

Strains of Rodrigo's *Concierto d'Aranjuez* filled the room as Nate came to sit opposite her. Kathryn had always liked the guitar concerto and closed her eyes, hearing the music as its blind composer must have done. But as the music went on, came to a passage that was so beautiful in its haunting sound, it so tugged at her that, never more happy with Nate so near, she just had to keep her eyes closed so he shouldn't know she was on the brink of emotional tears. Not tears of sadness, but tears from the pure golden sensitivity of the moment.

The haunting passage ended, and as it did so she heard Nate move, felt him near and opened her eyes to see he had come to sit on the arm of her chair. And she was too emotionally involved then to hide what she felt for him. And suddenly there was triumph in his eyes, triumph she didn't understand until very gently he pulled her to her feet.

'I've just learned,' he said softly, 'that the way to your heart is through music.' And she knew then he knew she loved him, that he knew and was not unhappy about it. Which could only mean, couldn't it—that he—that he loved her in return!

She smiled at him, and although she didn't think he was a shy man recalled he had said that once a Kingersby gave his heart it was for ever, so it had to be, hadn't it, that Nate had never said those words 'I love you', and could, her mind drifted dreamily on, mean he was having difficulty in getting the words out.

'You've had a hard day,' he told her gently, taking her unfinished glass of sherry from her. 'I think it's time you went to bed, don't you?'

'Yes,' she said, almost trancelike, her voice barely audible, knowing if she was dreaming then she never wanted to wake up as Nate put an arm around her and took her with him to switch off the tape, then went with her to guide her up the stairs and to the door of her room.

And there, with his arm still about her, he placed a warm kiss on her inviting mouth, looked as though it was hell to tear himself away, but found the will to remove his arm, saying softly:

'Goodnight, my beautiful Kathryn. I must leave you now, but I hope it won't always be like this.'

She had felt cold, forlorn, when he had removed his arm, but at his words heat enveloped her. And, her heart thudding, she just knew she couldn't let him go until she knew exactly what that remark meant.

'You want to—stay?' she enquired, pink staining her cheeks.

Nate's lips curved. 'Don't doubt it, my dear. But I think we'll have the wedding first . . .'

That was as far as he got. He hadn't told her he loved her, but he was asking her to marry him and at that moment the thought of actually being his wife entirely consumed her.

'Oh, Nate!' she cried, and couldn't help but fling herself at him, her arms going round him, who moved to kiss whom first immaterial as their lips met.

Met and clung, so that the fire that was in her for him went completely beyond her control, and nothing else mattered. How could it? Nate had asked her to marry him!

Rapturously she pressed herself to him, felt his hands at the back of her pulling her even closer, and gave him her whole heart when his kiss deepened.

Kiss for kiss she gave him, delighting when his hands caressed her, her hands gripping him in an ecstasy of rejoicing. Her love for him merged with a growing desire, a desire she knew had started to rage in him too.

And when their next kiss broke and Nate pulled back, showing all the signs that this was where he would say goodnight and mean it, she saw then that with him saying, 'I think we'll have the wedding first', he was struggling against his need for her.

But she didn't want him to go. She could not bear in those initial minutes of knowing her love returned that he should so soon leave her. And she clung on to him, pressed herself close up to him again, and to her joy heard the groan that escaped him before his voice thick with desire, he said:

'I want you, Kathryn. God help me, I want you,' just as though he was going through some mental torment.

And then they were in her room, the door closed, a trail of clothes leading to the bed as they kissed and parted, kissed and clung. And she felt no shame in the darkness that when Nate picked her up and placed her on the bed, her lips meeting his when he joined her, that she should feel only joy and ardour when their uncovered bodies touched. She was too lost in the wonder of this being what true love between a man and a woman meant—no inhibitions, no holding back.

CHAPTER EIGHT

DAWN was breaking when Kathryn awoke. She opened her eyes to find she had the wide double bed to herself. There were so many things she had to learn about Nate, she mused, a smile touching the corners of her mouth as she reflected that she had already discovered two things about him since they had entered this room last night—one, that he was a very tender lover, the other that he must be a very early riser.

She wondered if he had risen early so as to make a start on the work they had to do, get most of it out of the way so they could spend the rest of the day in the pure bliss of each other's company without work intruding on their new love.

Her smile deepened as her mind went back to his tenderness, his gentleness with her last night. Not that it had started out that way. There had been white-hot passion about him, a passion that drove him to possess her, a passion she had done her best in her uninitiated way to match.

She recalled how desire had ridden him, then the naked shock that had ripped through him as he discovered he was her first lover, the agony in him as he had tried to tear himself from her. But she hadn't allowed that. She had been so stirred to want him, she couldn't bear that he might find the strength to leave her. She had wrapped her arms tightly round him, begging him, 'Please, please don't leave me like this,' had caressed his bare skin and heard his demented cry as he had called out, 'Oh God!' and kissed her fiercely for long minutes before changing the tempo of his lovemaking to suit her untried body.

She had no idea of the time. Her watch had stopped, which wasn't surprising, she thought, since she had been in no mind to wind it up last night.

But suddenly she was in a fever of impatience to see him again. She was out of bed, bathing and dressing, the thought in her mind that if Nate was already at work then the sooner she lent him her pair of hands the sooner they would be through. They would talk today, she thought, as nothing but happiness in her heart she tripped lightly down the stairs.

The study when she opened the door was just as she and Nate had left it last night. No sign of him or that he had been anywhere near his study this morning. Happiness still in every step, Kathryn quietly opened the sitting room door on her way kitchenwards. And it was there that she saw Nate. The back of him anyway, for he was so deep in thought as he stared out of the window, he hadn't heard her.

Her spirits higher than they had ever been, it crossed her mind to tiptoe over to him to reach up and put her hands over his eyes and whisper, 'Guess who?' But sudden remembrance of the way they had been with each other brought an unexpected shyness to her.

'Hello, darling,' she said softly instead, staying near the door. She saw Nate jerk at the sound of her voice, and thinking only to wait to see his face, to see his smile before she rushed into his arms, stood waiting for him to turn around.

Strangely his hands were now clenched at his sides, she saw, but she shrugged aside whatever that might mean as she anticipated his loving smile as he began to turn.

But there was no smile on his face as he turned to face her. And as she took in that his expression was more *un*loving than she had ever seen it, she had the most dreadful premonition that something was terribly, terribly wrong. For the expression he wore was harsh, and though she just couldn't believe it, her eyes were reading that he was back to being that awful man she had first known!

No question of moving forward into his arms now, as her brain scooted off in all directions; had she been too forward last night? Had he received bad news about Rex? Fearing the latter, she just had to ask:

'Darling, what's wrong?' and heard none of the loving gentleness she had been expecting as he grated harshly:

'Why the *hell* didn't you tell me you were a virgin before I became too—involved to stop?'

His way of speaking to her shocked her, when she had been anticipating a very different tone. And then she saw the reason for it. Other women he might take to his bed, but the girl he intended to marry was someone special—he had intimated as much by saying he wanted them to be married first.

'I love you, Nate,' she said, saying the only thing she could that would make him see nothing else mattered.

But that didn't appear to have helped things at all, as she saw from the way his jaw was working. He didn't need her declaration of love at this point. Her voice becoming hesitant now, she tried again to get him to see that she had given herself to him willingly, that before or after marriage didn't matter when she loved him so completely.

'Loving you,' she said, 'it—it didn't seem important to tell . . .'

'*Important*!' he ground out before she could finish. 'Of course it's *bloody* important! You know damn well I thought Rex had been your lover.'

She would have thought he would be glad she hadn't physically been with his brother, and her bewilderment showed as she asked, 'It makes a difference that he hasn't?'

'*God*!' Nate exploded. 'Can't you see why? Can't you see this whole mess is based on lies?'

'Lies?' she repeated, dumbfounded, too stunned by his

attitude being so different from what she had thought it would be to take in what he was trying to tell her.

'Of course lies,' Nate said, and Kathryn wasn't sure then who he was growing more furious with, her or himself, as he flung at her, 'Can't you see yet that every time I was the least bit pleasant to you it was false? Are you so dumb you don't know I've planned to make you pay from the very beginning?'

'Make me pay?' she whispered, stupefied.

'I looked for a way to make you suffer the way you'd made my brother suffer,' he threw at her. 'I watched you for days trying to see what made you tick. I watched to find out where you were most vulnerable.' And while she was still gasping in disbelief, wanting to cry, no, no, that it couldn't be so, that he must be making it up, he was going on, looking as though he was hating himself every bit as much as he was hating her, 'I found what I was looking for the day your sister rang, the day you went to spend the weekend with her. Infidelity was your weak spot.' And not flinching from the truth, he told her, 'In seconds I had my plan worked out.'

It wasn't ice that entered Kathryn's heart as she stood unable to move, stood and was made to believe him—believe as the dreadful words he was saying began to sink in that this time another Kingersby had shattered her love. Nate had sworn to avenge his brother, had sworn he would get even with her that Rex had only just escaped being crippled for life. And as she began to see that Nate Kingersby had deliberately set out to make her fall in love with him—just for the satisfaction of seeing how she felt when she was thrown over—there was no room in her as anger began slowly to kindle inside her for ice to form. Nate had brought up the word infidelity, and she started to see then, even as part of her mind still couldn't believe it, that on that very afternoon when his manner had so suddenly changed and he had suggested they bury their bone of contention while at the office, he had planned to break her the way he thought she had broken his brother.

'You're saying you never intended marrying me, is that right?' she questioned tautly, knowing that must be the truth, but finding she needed to hear it from his own lips. Even now she needed to have it said, needed to know the mockery of love last night had been confirmed.

'I planned to be engaged to you for a very short while,' Nate agreed, the light where he was standing giving his face a grey look as he didn't back away from telling her the truth, 'But I had no intention of marrying you.'

That hurt, cut right to the heart of her, but she bore that hurt, invited more as she voiced the next question her intelligence had brought.

'You wanted me to suffer the way Rex had suffered. Did that include arranging the wedding?'

'Yes,' he answered stiffly.

'But you were going to jilt me a week before the wedding?'

She knew the answer was yes, and didn't understand why Nate shook his head in reply. Until, like a bolt from the blue, it came to her that her fate was to be far worse than that.

'You must hate me,' she said, anger momentarily dying at the knife thrust of pain with which that knowledge was received. 'You weren't going to tell me the wedding was off at all, were you?' she challenged, pain blunted as anger, fury spurted into life. 'You were intending that I should arrive at the church, but that you wouldn't, weren't you?' And too angry now at the picture that evoked to think of sparing him, not seeing any reason why she should after the humiliation he had planned for her, 'Or were you going to go one better than that, since it's *infidelity* we're talking of?'

'One better . . .?' Nate broke in, that he had no idea what she was meaning obvious.

But Kathryn was too fired up to want to hear anything he had to say. 'Perhaps you planned a Kingersby repeat performance,' she flared, ignoring that he had started to look angry too. 'Perhaps you were going to let me have a key to this house so I could move my things in the way Rex gave me a key to his flat,' she rushed on. 'Perhaps you were going to give me the Friday afternoon off the way your uncle did. Only unlike your brother you would know what I planned to do with that afternoon, wouldn't you?'

'What the hell are you talking about?' Nate bit at her sharply. But Kathryn, having lost her temper, ignored him.

'Perhaps you were going to arrange for me to come down here with all my bits and pieces, fool myself into thinking, as I did when I took my things over to your brother's home, that it would be amusing for my fiancé to find one of my dresses hanging beside something of his in his wardrobe. Was I to find, the way I did when I went breezing into Rex's bedroom, that my adoring *new* fiancé was in bed with another woman?'

'*What*!' The ringing exclamation that broke from him had her faltering, her fury abating. But it was only temporary as Nate got over his shock and said hoarsely, 'I don't believe it.'

And that was the final straw as far as Kathryn was concerned—that even now, when if he thought about it, he must know Rex had lied, Nate still wasn't ready to believe her. And there was a note of hysteria entering her anger as she challenged, her voice rising:

'Go and see him. Go and ask him about his secretary. According to Maxine Vernon, when she'd had the decency to put something on before she came to where I was giving Rex back his ring, it wasn't the first time.'

'I can't—believe it.' She saw his colour wasn't grey as he stepped away from the window and towards her, it was white.

Afraid he was going to touch her, Kathryn stepped back. But she had no need to retreat farther as Nate, a couple of yards from her, came to a halt, shaking his head as though to clear it.

'I need to think,' he said after a moment. And, decisive again as she knew him to be, 'I'm going for a walk. We'll talk when I get back.' And as though the thoughts already raging in his head were too much with her in the same room, without another word he strode past her.

The door had hardly closed behind him before Kathryn was haring up the stairs to pack. Like hell we'll talk! she thought furiously, stuffing things any old how inside her case. She had heard enough from him to last her a lifetime. Had he not discovered that no other man had touched her he would not have told her anything, she saw that clearly enough.

Well, I hope it hangs like lead on your conscience, Mr Nate Seducer Kingersby! she thought as she snapped the lock shut on her case. But by the time she had made it to her car, tears were falling like rain down her face, for she loved him so much it had been a mutual seduction.

Her vision blinded, she mopped furiously at her tears as she headed back to London. A visit to Reading out of the question, for unlike that other time when her world had fallen apart, this was something she couldn't share with another soul, not even her sister.

Kathryn had all that day to mourn for her futile dreams, all that day to call Nate Kingersby every name she could think of and still have time to discover that no matter how evil his intent, no matter how her love had been shaken, it was still there—she still loved the swine.

Pride, she thought when she got up the next morning and looked at red eyes that were going to call for all her artistry with her cosmetics. Pride was her most valued possession that Monday morning.

She knew very well Nate wouldn't expect her at the office. But she was going, if only to hand in her notice. After all, she had done nothing wrong—but lose her virtue, she thought, refusing to give way to fresh tears. And if, as she had concluded yesterday, the only reason all this had come out was because he had been devastated to find she had been a virgin when his brother had as good as told him otherwise, then for the next month until her notice was worked out she hoped, if Nate Kingersby had a conscience at all, that every time he clapped eyes on her, his conscience would give him hell.

A month, she thought, of having to face the ache in her heart was about all she would be able to put up with herself. And even George Kingersby wouldn't keep her to her promise to stay the full three months if he knew what had transpired.

She had her resignation all ready, typed out on her portable last night. But even with pride ramrod-stiff, she had to swallow before, lifting her head a fraction and keeping it held high, she walked into the office.

Nate Kingersby got no good morning from her that morning. But she didn't miss his astonishment as he rose from his chair, when without pausing to stop at her desk she extracted the envelope from her bag as she sailed into his office. Slapping the envelope down on his desk, Kathryn would have sailed straight out again, had not his voice stopped her.

'Your resignation?' His voice was even, his expression sombre now his astonishment had left him.

'Got it in one,' she said shortly, just the sight of him weakening her proud resolve to show him no man was going to walk all over her and think he had seen her off with her tail between her legs. She brought proud backbone to bear, standing defiantly there when her aching heart would have had her bolting for the cloakroom.

'A month?' Nate queried.

'It's all that's required,' she told him now she was over her weak moment, and wondering how she would keep from hitting him if under the circumstances he so much as mentioned her promise to his uncle.

Then she saw his shrewd eyes were on hers and didn't wait for him to say anything, wanting to distract his observant eyes from seeing the evidence of the floods of tears she had wept yesterday.

'That is unless you intend to dismiss me on the spot for . . .' She stopped, went a fiery red, and would have fled then as she realised there were no words to describe the nothing-held-back way she had given her full self to him. But into her agitated mind came the chord of remembrance to remind her she had gone to his home to work ' for industrial misconduct,' she said, and feeling better when she saw the way he didn't like what she told him, 'And I wouldn't put that past a vindictive Kingersby!'

They stood facing each other, Nate towering over her. He didn't like what she said, she could see that. But whatever he was feeling he controlled it, and raised a hand as though to touch her. But she knew what his touch could do to her and stepped out of range. Then she saw any anger she had pricked in him by her slur on the Kingersby clan had gone when he mistook her reason for backing away.

'I can't blame you for not wanting me to touch you after the way I've behaved,' he said quietly. 'As for dismissing you,' he broke off, then his voice deadly serious, 'you can have no idea, Kathryn, how very much I admire you for coming into the office at all, considering the wrongs we Kingersbys have dealt you.'

Having the way she had reviled the Kingersbys handed back to her made void anything else she might have to say about his family, put her on the defensive when she didn't want to be defensive—and that made her mad.

'My God,' she stormed, 'that's big of you!'

'You're not going to allow me to apologise, are you?' he said, and she could see his eyes were beginning to glint dangerously. But she didn't care, as she saw just why he was so ready to apologise.

'So you're ready to believe what I told you yesterday, are you?' she said heatedly, and following up with what she knew must be true, scorned, 'I'm honoured! Did it take you long to get the truth out of Rex when you went to see him?' It was for sure he wouldn't have believed her without going to have his brother confirm it for him.

'I haven't seen Rex since Friday,' Nate shook her by saying, and that glint in his eyes exploded into anger suddenly. 'Hell, do you think I need more proof than you showed me on Saturday night to know he deliberately misled me? Even without remembering how barren your flat looked that first time I visited you, barren because you hadn't had time yet to set out again the things you'd taken with you to my brother's flat—do you think I need more proof than Saturday to know I could believe you in preference to him? Good God, woman,' he raged, 'don't you realise how sick to my gut I feel at what I've done?'

'Good,' said Kathryn, not seeing why he shouldn't suffer if he was to be believed, and was inwardly flailing himself. 'I hope it keeps you awake at night!' And with that she marched back to her office.

But the way they were with each other as the week dragged on didn't make for a good working atmosphere. Nate had tried to apologise, but she hadn't let him, and now he had taken to being aloofly polite but no more.

And from her own point of view she just couldn't be natural with him. He had used her, she thought bitterly, and wanted to shrivel up and hide when she recalled the way she had so naïvely told him she loved him.

Determined that by the time she left he would be in no

doubt whatsoever that not only did she no longer love him, but that hatred had grown in love's place, Kathryn hardened her heart, so that even though there were still moments when she would look up and find him watching her, moments when no longer any insincere smile came her way, she would remember her resolve that he should know she hated him, and if she had the chance before he looked away, she would look straight through him.

But as the week dawdled to a close, her resolve to show him nothing but hate began to weaken. Only that morning she had caught herself ready to smile at him when, his own aloofness dropping, he had said something pleasant to her. She had managed to check her smile, but had become so fed up with herself that when lunchtime came she was glad to get out.

Why couldn't she hate him? she wondered as she window-shopped without interest, not interested in lunch either. He didn't deserve any less. Oh, how she wished she could get him out of her mind, out of her head! With an effort she concentrated on the display in the window of a dress shop her feet had halted at. That's a nice dress, she thought without enthusiasm. Then she looked again and saw it was a really lovely dress. It was made of some sort of crêpey material, of pastel colours, pale shades of blue all merging. Why not? she thought, ignoring the fact that she didn't need anything new. She needed cheering up, didn't she?

She went in and tried it on, and couldn't resist it when she saw how beautifully it suited her. Sophistication and simplicity were combined in the short-sleeved dress with its tie belt and flaring hemline. The weather was getting warmer now. At a pinch she could get away with wearing it to the office, for all it was a shade too dressy for that, she thought, visions of Nate's eyes popping when he saw her decked out in it. The vision faded as, annoyed with herself, she despaired that her thoughts went back to him time and time again.

'I'll take it,' she told the waiting salesgirl, who hadn't had to stress that the dress must have been made for her.

Kathryn was late getting back to the office by some twenty minutes, and saw when she went in that Nate was in her room, the frown on his brow clearing when he saw her.

'I thought something had happened to you,' he said, checking his watch, sounding anxious to her ears and causing her to think ridiculously that he had been nursing the same fears she had that day he had come in late, that day she had fretted in case he had had an accident.

Idiot! she calmed the way her heart had acted at the mere thought he might be concerned in case some reckless driver had knocked her over in her lunch hour. But the wild thought, ridiculous though it was, that he did care about her in some small way had taken from her the coolness that had been with her all week.

'Sorry I'm late,' she delivered the courtesy that was due to him as her employer, and held her paper carrier aloft.

'You've been having a spend,' said Nate, and slowly that smile, that genuine smile that was separate from that insincere half smile that had frequently come her way in the past, warmed his face.

'I don't really deserve another new dress,' she said, her smile coming involuntarily. Her wardrobe was packed with her trousseau.

'You deserve everything you want,' said Nate, his tone serious, his smile disappearing.

Kathryn's own smile faded, and hurt started to show in her eyes as abruptly she turned away. Cool again, she stooped to put down her purchase.

'I got more than I deserved from both the Kingersby brothers, didn't I?' she said bitterly.

She didn't expect him to answer, but stayed fiddling with her parcel so she needn't have to meet his eyes in the seconds of silence that stretched—and only straightened when, without saying another word, Nate went to his own office.

She would have to stop this bitterness from welling up every time he was nice to her, she thought, as over the weekend she kept herself as busy as she could in an ineffectual effort to stop herself from thinking about him. It was her self-defence mechanism at work, she knew that. But, recalling the way she had spoken to him on Friday, she felt there had been a hint to it of self-pity.

By Monday she had come to terms with herself. Men for her were out. So too was self-pity. She had been hurt, and would hurt for a long time, she faced that. But she wasn't going to let that hurt spoil her life, feed the bitterness she felt, until she ended up some dried-up old spinster.

'Good morning,' she greeted Nate when she went into work. Although there was no smile in her voice, she had come a long way from last week when not once had she offered him a greeting.

And so the week began. And as it progressed she saw that if she had been too full of the thoughts of Nate's treachery to be barely civil to him last week, then he too had been too shaken by what had been revealed to be his true self last week too. And by the time Friday came again, she knew that she hadn't fallen mistakenly in love with a man who because of the part he had been playing didn't exist. She had seen a new side to Nate that week, a side that showed him courteous, pleasant and considerate, a man who treated her with respect. And she had to be glad she had handed in her resignation, because she had fallen more in love with him than ever.

He had been out for some part of that afternoon, and having nothing very much on hand to keep her attention from wandering, by the time he returned Kathryn had realised that if she didn't do something about her heart that didn't seem to know it was wasting its time in loving Nate, she had better start being cool to him again. For every warm remark he made had been replied to with a thawing of her coldness towards him, so that if she was to leave in a fortnight's time without crying all over him, then she had better do something about that thaw right now.

'Been busy?' he enquired, coming in and stopping at her desk, his eyes taking in that she had no smile for him.

'Not particularly,' she answered coolly, and watched as his eyes narrowed at her change of attitude and added, not knowing what she was going to say if he questioned the change, 'I've put the telephone messages I've taken on your desk.' And she could have jumped for joy when the phone on her desk rang and required her attention.

Not once did she look through the doorway of the two offices in the hour that was to follow until five, though it had taken an enormous effort of will many many times not to do so. And it was on the stroke of five, not sure her nerves would take much more, that she threw the cover over her typewriter, flung Nate a hasty though still cool, 'Goodnight,' and raced to the car park.

She was still sitting in her car five minutes later wishing she had done something about having it seen to when it had acted up this morning. Again she tried to start the wretched thing, then to her chagrin she felt a coolness on her legs as the car door was opened, and heard Nate say smoothly:

'You'll have to get that thing seen to, Kathryn, won't you?'

'I will, won't I?' she answered woodenly.

'Meantime,' he drawled, 'my services as a chauffeur are at your disposal.'

'I . . .' she began, ready to refuse, then read something in his eyes that told her he had had enough of her freezing him out this past hour, and that if she couldn't rise above being small-minded and accept his offer of a lift in the spirit it was given, then he didn't think much of her. 'Thank you,' she said with cool politeness.

She was bowling along in his car before it came to her to wonder why she should want his good opinion anyway. What was it to her that Nate should think well of her after what he had done? Oh, how could she love such a ruthless, coldhearted man? she mourned, and tried to keep up her cool pose when memory came of how wonderful he had been all week.

As if he knew that any attempt he made at conversation would be replied to with only monosyllabic answers, Nate, to her annoyance, spoke not a word, but drove at a steady rate, stern-faced, until they turned into the avenue where she lived.

About to leave the car with the briefest of farewells, Kathryn was stopped by Nate speaking for the first time in what seemed an age.

'I know any apology from me in no way makes up for the hurt I've caused you, Kathryn,' he said, never more serious. 'But are you anywhere near ready yet to believe how bitterly I regret what happened?'

'Why should I be?' she fired back, pride out in front in not wanting him to know that hurt was still a raw wound of heart bleeding hurt.

'Because,' he said slowly, very deliberately, his hand coming to capture one of hers as if suspecting she might shoot away from him, just his touch telling her she had a fight on her hands if she didn't want to give in, whatever it was, 'Because,' he repeated, 'I should very much like to start off afresh.' And when she would have jerked her hand out of his, he kept his hold firm, insisting she hear him out. 'I should like to take you out—to dinner or anywhere else you'd like to go.' Again she struggled to free her hand, but found he had no intention of releasing her.

'Your guilty conscience is showing!' she erupted, coolness

deserting her the longer she could feel his touch on her skin.

He took her scorn with equanimity. 'It has nothing to do with my conscience, guilty or otherwise,' he told her evenly. Then he paused and said, hiding nothing, 'I feel I know you a little, Kathryn, but I should like you to get to know me better.'

Anger soared in her, reached a peak, and she was glad of it as she blazed, 'In my view we know each other far too well as it is!' Her face went scarlet, but she was too furious to back down. 'You led me falsely once before, Nate Kingersby—never again, thanks very much!'

'It wouldn't be false this time,' he told her, a world of sincerity in his voice. And oddly, she thought, Nate, whom she had never known have difficulty in finding just the right words, seemed to be having a hard time finding the right words just then. 'Come out with me, Kathryn,' he urged at last. 'Never again will I deceive you, believe me,' and, his hand gripping hers, 'There's—something I want to tell you, but I'll never be able to unless you're prepared to meet me part of the way.'

He was getting to her so that she so nearly gave in, so nearly let her heart rule her head and tell him she would go out with him. Then remembering the way she had met him more than part of the way once, she felt anger again at the weak-kneed creature he made her.

'Anything you want to tell me can be said right here,' she said shortly, and witnessed the glint in his eyes that told her he was growing angry that she was too muleheaded to go along that path to meet him.

'This isn't the appropriate time or place,' he rapped back, his anger starting to burn.

'No?' she queried loftily. 'When would be the appropriate time, Nate?' Her anger fed on memories that were now far from beautiful. 'What place do you suggest? Your place in Surrey? In one of the bedrooms? What is it you want to tell me? Something you forgot to tell me when I gave myself freely, innocently, not knowing the only truth about a Kingersby is that you can't believe a thing they say?' Her sudden fury was in no way finished even though she could see she had fired a similar fury in him. 'Anything you want to tell me, Nate Kingersby, can be said here and now. I'd die before I'd go anywhere with you again!'

She had stung him, as she had meant to. But as the hold on his temper broke and furious words left him, she was so stunned by what those words were that for several seconds she just couldn't say a thing.

'Dammit, woman,' he roared, 'I want to tell you I'll marry you!'

All colour left her face as those words rocketed round the car, the words chasing around in her brain until she found her voice.

'You'll marry me?' she repeated, stunned.

Then as slowly her world righted itself she saw in a flash the only reason he could have for making such a statement, and her fury boiled over. It gave her the sheer brute force needed to snatch her hand away from him, had her opening the car door before he could know what she was about.

'You'll marry me,' she repeated again, and had one last thing to say before she raced indoors. 'Like hell you will! A rattlesnake has got more chance!'

CHAPTER NINE

CHARGING up the stairs, fingers all thumbs as she found her door key and fumbled it into the lock, haste of the utmost importance lest Nate had charged after her, Kathryn entered her sitting room and slammed the door shut—and didn't breathe freely again until her ears told her in the sound of his car drawing away, that Nate wasn't coming after her.

He would have got short shrift if he had anyway, she thought, still furious with him. How dared he say, just like that, 'I'll marry you'? Just as though he thought it the only honourable thing he thought he could do! Let him stew with his conscience.

Who did he think he was, anyway, that in this day and age he could treat her like some compromised Victorian maid? To so magnanimously let her know he intended to pay for what he had done. It infuriated her that to right the wrong inflicted by leading her to believe he had marriage in mind when she had given herself to him, he was now condescending to offer to marry her. She'd see him hang first!

Tears came as her anger cooled. Tears he wasn't worth, she sniffed, as determined not to cry any more she pottered about her flat—and had cause to dab at her eyes again at the thought that there hadn't been any conditions attached to the love she gave him; her love to him had been given unconditionally.

She was dry-eyed the next morning when she phoned the garage about her car, only to find her confidence that they would do what they had to to her dynamo and have it ready to be collected within a few hours showed how little she knew of the motor repair business.

'We're chock-a-block,' the service man told her. 'Can't do it this weekend.' He then went into detail about a five-day week, told her his men would be working overtime next week as it was, and when she finally pinned him down to say when he could have her car in he said, making sucking noises, 'Bring it in—um—a week on Monday. If you bring it in early it'll be ready for you some time in the afternoon.'

'Can you get it going today?' Kathryn enquired, crossing her fingers that he could help her out as he had the last time, and a minute later was able to uncross her fingers as after a little humming and hawing he said that he could.

When later she went to pick up the Mini, she was in no hurry to get home. In no hurry to do anything any more, she mused, as she stopped at a bookshop and spent an age choosing a couple of paperbacks. Perhaps if she was lucky she might be able to lose herself in their pages tonight, she thought hopefully, and then went home.

It was late afternoon when she was in the middle of getting her ironing board out to do some small bits of ironing that the phone rang. She hoped it was Fay. She had thought of ringing her, but after cancelling their arrangements to go to the cinema that time she didn't feel up to any of her remarks if Fay ribbed her about it.

It wasn't Fay. And she would know those deep, well accented tones anywhere! He didn't have to say the, 'Nate', that followed his, 'Hello, Kathryn,' for her to know who it was, the weakness in her limbs confirming what her ears were telling her.

'This is an unexpected pleasure,' she said, trying for acid, but her anger was absent; his call was so unforeseen she was not ready to deal with it.

His voice was level as he replied, pretending to believe her, 'Thought I might cheer your day.'

Her lips firmed. 'What do you want, Nate?' she asked

abruptly, and would not have been at all surprised in the silence that followed to have the phone slammed down on her for her rudeness.

But Nate did not slam down the phone. And his voice was still level when eventually he said, 'I want you to have dinner with me tonight.'

'No, thanks.' It didn't need thinking about.

'Why won't you?' he had the limitless nerve to ask, then had her fighting not to slam the phone down on him and thereby let him know the accuracy of his shot when he asked slowly, 'Are you afraid to?'

Afraid? Oh yes, she was afraid. Afraid he would discover she still loved him. Afraid because she just knew that despite her pride, if she were to spend several hours with him, their talk unconnected with work, that charm of his in action, then he would soon learn that she didn't feel anywhere near as cool about him as she was trying to make out.

'Why should I be afraid?' she asked, and not wanting to hear what had made him suggest she might be, from somewhere dredged up an uncaring laugh. 'Good grief, Nate! It's getting on for five in the afternoon. Do you seriously imagine yours is the first phone call I've had today?'

She had to give him full marks for not being slow on the uptake, as quickly he came back, 'You already have a date for this evening?'

'It would appear that I'm in everyone's little black book,' she replied airily. 'You really will have to get yours started, Nate, if it's me you have to call every time you're at a loose end.' Not that she believed any longer that she had been the only girl he could think of to take to the Atkins' dinner party. It had all been part of his plan to . . .

'Who is he?' The question came sharply, ignoring her jibe, and throwing her for a moment that he should have such massive cheek to think he had any right to know.

'That's my business,' she snapped in return, and couldn't resist saying before she put the phone down, 'Though I can tell you this much, Nate, he's a man I know I can trust absolutely not to feed me a load of lies!'

She should have felt better than she did for having said that, she thought, wishing he had never called to unsettle her. But she didn't feel better. She felt mean for having turned the knife when he had told her, that Monday following, that what he had done made him sick to his gut.

On Monday, unsure whether she was going to throw Nate a greeting or not, she found herself having to reply when he got in first with, 'Good morning, Kathryn, pleasant weekend?'

'Good morning,' she said, and let him think the smile that tugged from her was not from the pure pleasure of seeing him, but was on account of the weekend she had just spent. 'Super,' she added, seeing his eyes were on her mouth, and that he couldn't help noticing the way it curved happily.

He was frowning when he raised his eyes to hers. 'Well, let's hope you're not too exhausted to put your back into it today,' he said sourly.

'That's not fair! she flew back at him. 'When have I ever not done my job properly? Even after that . . .' She came to a full stop, biting her lip at what she had been going to say.

Then she found Nate knew anyway. For, his expression changing, he came up to her. 'Even after that time when you were hurt so badly you spent the night weeping,' he said gently, doing nothing to stiffen her resistance to his tone by bringing up a warm hand to cup the side of her face. 'It *was* an unfair remark, Kathryn—forgive me. But . . .'

Suddenly the door opened, and they both turned, her action moving Nate's hand from her as unhurriedly he let it drop to his side.

'Mr Kingersby!' she exclaimed, and had to forget her

own feelings, gladness surging up as she saw a tanned and much fitter looking George Kingersby standing there.

'Can't leave the place alone, can you?' Nate was saying to his uncle, going over and shaking him warmly by the hand. 'When did you get back?'

'Yesterday,' said George. 'I just thought I'd pop in to see if everything was going all right for the celebrations on Wednesday.' And while Kathryn was wondering how she had ever thought her face would be one that would be missing when the firm celebrated its fifty years of existence on Wednesday, he turned to her and said, 'The new chairman treating you all right, eh?'

Which left her fumbling to find an answer while wondering if he had seen the way Nate's hand had been against her cheek. 'I—I'm glad to see you,' she said, and left it at that, not looking at Nate as George beamed, then went through to the other room with Nate, the door closing for the first time since George had vacated that office.

Had she not seen George again, the thoughts she had had of avoiding the celebrations would she was sure have been acted upon: there would be so many people there she wouldn't be missed anyway, her thoughts had gone. But seeing him again, remembering the happy way he had beamed at her, she felt an unwanted weakening; and had to wonder, then, would George of whom she had grown fond, be terribly offended if he did happen to notice her absence?

Quietly she got on with some work, her watch ticking up that he had been in with Nate for over an hour. Of course they would have a lot to discuss. Business mainly, and George would want to tell Nate all about his holiday.

She was on the point of wondering if she should have some coffee sent in to them or alternatively would Nate ring through and ask for some if he wanted it, when the door opened and they both came out, Nate courteously escorting his uncle through her office. She looked up as George came near to her desk, a warm natural smile for him on her lips.

But her smile faded when she saw how George was looking at her. She wondered for a moment if Nate had possibly told him she was the worst secretary he had ever had. For George's eyes were so troubled, she just knew something had been said about her.

Then, 'Kathryn my dear,' the old man said, 'what can I say? What can I do to make it up to you?'

'Make it up . . .?' She had no idea what he was talking about.

'Nate has just finished telling me the reason why you broke off your engagement to Rex,' he said sorrowfully.

'He did *what*!' she exclaimed, her eyes flying indignantly to Nate. 'How could you?' she asked him, seeing from the unrepentant look of him that he could, easily.

But George was speaking again, telling her, 'Had Nate bothered to have a word with me on the subject first, although there wasn't time for us to discuss anything but business before I went, I could have told him I'd learned enough about you to know you wouldn't have hurt Rex unless there was some exceptionally good reason.'

'Oh, Mr Kingersby!' she exclaimed, her heart full that he should think so well of her—and was then flabbergasted to find that that wasn't all Nate had acquainted his uncle with.

'Nate has also told me of the diabolical way he planned to make you pay for Rex still being in hospital.'

Scarlet covered every part of her. She could no longer look at George. She wouldn't look at Nate. That he could have told his uncle what had happened between them—! An insurmountable feeling of having been betrayed yet again threatened to have her crumbling.

'Will you forgive us for what we've done to you?' George asked.

And Kathryn was so taken aback that he should take his

family's guilt on his shoulders, that she just had to try and get a grip on herself. Especially when she recalled that George was the only one of them—remembering the way Tim and Jeremy had both cut her; not counting Nate's treachery—who had any sort of faith that she wouldn't have hurt Rex without cause.

'There's nothing to forgive you for,' she said, raising her eyes to look at him, 'honestly.'

He smiled as though he wanted to believe it. 'You will come to the celebrations on Wednesday, won't you?' he asked, seeming to know her better than she had thought.

'Wouldn't miss it,' she said, knowing now that she couldn't and trying to sound cheerful.

George didn't stay long after he had her confirmation, and Kathryn waited only until Nate had come away from the door after seeing his uncle through it and closing it, before she was rounding on him:

'How *could* you! How *could* you tell him about—about us?' she raged.

'If you're referring to the fact that we spent a night together,' Nate lost no time in bringing out into the open what was mortifying her, 'then stop worrying . . .'

'Stop worrying?' she burst in. 'Don't you have the least idea . . .'

'For God's sake,' Nate interrupted her, angry himself as he said, 'what the hell do you think I am.'

'You mean you don't *know*?' she fired bitterly, and saw he had taken a hold of his anger when, his voice calmer, he said:

'I told him about Rex purely because I wanted everyone in my family to know how entirely blameless you are. I told him what I'd planned for you because I don't consider I should be painted white either . . .'

'Well, I hope it makes you feel better, because . . .' she tried to get in.

'But I did not tell him about that night we shared because . . .'

'Because grey you didn't mind being painted, but black in your family's eyes was too . . .'

'Dammit, Kathryn,' he blazed, his hold on his temper gone, 'I don't care who the hell knows what a swine I was! But I respect your feelings too much to have everyone knowing . . .'

'How easily seduceable I am?' she jumped in.

She saw then that he had had enough, that he looked ready to explode. She saw from the way his jaw was working that he was striving for control. Then as if he knew that in the same office with her he didn't stand a chance of retrieving his short temper, he wheeled about and marched to his own office, banging the door tight shut before she could draw another breath.

A mood of hostility hung in the air for the rest of that day and all the following day, lingering over into Wednesday. But since Kathryn was now familiar with the way he worked, she had little reason to go in to see him. And from what she could make out he didn't want to see her more than he had to. For he no longer called her in to help him with anything, preferring to get through anything that needed checking on his own. So that apart from sitting in his office to take dictation it was about the only time she ventured in there. But it was on that Wednesday just as she was getting ready to go home that Nate came up to her.

'How are you getting to the hotel tonight?' he asked abruptly.

'I'm going in my car.'

'You've had it fixed?'

'The garage can't take it until Monday—it's having a new dynamo . . .'

'I'll take you,' he stated, just as though it was settled.

'No, you won't,' she came back promptly.

'It will be dark when you drive home. If your dynamo's on the blink it could let you down any time.'

'In that case I'll take a taxi,' she snapped, and didn't wait for him to blast her eardrums with some 'Dammit, woman, how are you going to get a taxi at that time of night?' remark.

She was rather pleased with her appearance, as thoughts she couldn't do anything about had her having a second look in her mirror before she left. Would Nate think she looked good in her wine-coloured silk with its snug fit? she couldn't stop from thinking—then felt suddenly angry with herself. What did she care what he thought?

There were many people at the hotel where the celebrations were being held whom she did not know, but also a good many whom, if not exactly knowing their names, she had a nodding acquaintance with. She entered the large ballroom, buffet tables laid all down one side, and stood in the doorway for a moment deciding where she would go.

But to her great surprise, and before she could make any movement to go to her left, Tim Kingersby, who only last week would have cut her dead had he had the chance, had appeared from nowhere and was blocking her path.

'We're all mixing in tonight after the speeches,' he said. 'But I would be more than pleased, Kathryn, if you would come and sit with us at the Kingersby table until we all start circulating.'

Finding she was made of sterner stuff than to take delight in cutting him in return, which she had to admit was tempting, Kathryn found herself replying, 'Thank you, Tim,' and refusing politely, 'But I've arranged to sit with one of the other secretaries.'

She knew then as Tim departed, and before she could move two steps Jeremy Kingersby came up to her with the same request, that word had got round the family about the way she had come upon Rex with Maxine Vernon.

She gave Jeremy the same answer she had given Tim. And it was not because she was piqued with the whole lot of them that she did so, but simply because she knew that wherever he was now, probably behind the scenes somewhere with George and his wife Dora, that very shortly Nate would be joining the Kingersby table. She looked round for any of the secretaries she knew and saw an empty chair by one of them.

Her sights in that direction, she was half way there, then felt a hand on her arm halting her. She had no need to look to see who it was; instinct had told her it was Nate before she looked up and met the grimness of his blue eyes.

'I've just received a deputation in the shape of two cousins who tell me you've disdained to sit with us,' he told her, not wasting his time on being agreeable, the only pleasantness about him being the curve of his mouth, purely she knew for the sake of anyone watching.

She allowed her own lips to curve, her eyes as cold as his. 'So,' she said, determined to show him she didn't care a hoot, that his hand on her arm didn't affect her in the slightest, 'what else is new?'

The curve left his mouth briefly as his eyes glinted. Then he was in control again, remembering they were standing where they could be observed. 'This,' he said, his voice arctic now for all the curve was back. 'I'm not asking you to join us, Kathryn, I'm telling you . . .'

'You're telling *me* . . .?' she started to retort, but found that this wasn't an occasion when Nate was going to let her have her say in any argument.

'I'm telling you,' he gritted quietly, 'that unless you want to upset my uncle by keeping up this unforgiving attitude, unless you want to put a blight on this evening he's looked forward to for a very long while, then if you're anything at all like the sensitive person I know you to be, you'll come with me now.'

He knew how to get to her, didn't he? she thought, the smell of defeat already being breathed in. Nate knew full well that by suggesting that his uncle would be upset he had pulled the rug of choice from under her feet.

'Your uncle might not want me to , . .' she tried futilely.

'He'll be very hurt if you don't.'

Quietly she gave in. 'Very well,' she said—and soon saw, the second he had got his way, how the hard look left Nate, and how that pretence of a smile changed into a genuine one.

But she couldn't deny the thrill she felt at crossing the room with his hand firmly clasping her elbow, nor the pleasure that went through her when, as if one, all the Kingersby men, Adrian on a flying visit with his pretty wife, still pleasantly plump after having her baby, Paul over from France, Jeremy and Tim, all stood up as they neared.

'Sit by me,' said Paul at once, he of them all having the most blatant roving eye, and pulling out a chair for her when Nate let go of her arm.

Never having expected to enjoy the evening, as everyone assembled, drinks passed round and the speeches began, Kathryn began to unwind and realise that if she let herself she could have a very agreeable time in the hours before she drove herself home.

Tim, Paul, Jeremy and Adrian all got up to make a short speech, and then it was Nate's turn. And she thought he looked so wonderful standing there, making his audience laugh with some witticism pertaining to their industry, that she had frequently to look away just in case of the remote possibility that someone was looking at her, not at him, and would see the love she had for him in her face.

The reference she expected him to make regarding the one member of the board who was not present came in the shape of Nate saying how well his brother was doing, and how before the year was out he would be back with them as fit as he had been before his accident.

She was truly glad Rex was getting on so well, that he would be back at work by the end of the year, but was saddened for a moment as she wondered where she would be by that time. Then she had to lift herself, for Nate had handed over to George, who looked across at their table and smiled as he spotted her, his eyes travelling on to his wife, before he started.

Once the speeches were out of the way hilarity broke out, as George wanted. The dance band hired for the evening began to play, and George and his wife did one circuit before coming off the floor and going over to talk to people. A few brave souls sauntered to the buffet first and soon everyone appeared to be all arms and elbows going for the food. But no one else seemed to want to take the floor until someone else got up to dance.

'Can I get you something, Kathryn?'

Nate's voice had her looking to see that somehow, when only a minute before Paul had been seated next to her, it was Nate who now occupied that chair.

'Not for the moment,' she replied, conscious how his eyes were on her face, on her dress.

'In that case, shall we dance?' And as if suspecting she was about to refuse, 'Someone has to show the way.'

She didn't want to be in his arms; she knew herself too vulnerable to his touch. But hearing it put like that, Nate including her in the duties the Kingersbys had to perform to make the evening a success, she got to her feet.

It was heaven, as she knew it would be. Nate was a good dancer, but it would have been the same had he not been. For moments neither of them spoke. Kathryn was trying all she could to concentrate on the beat of the music, trying not to lose herself in this short time of having Nate's arm around her, his hand holding hers.

Other couples began to come on to the floor and she felt

Nate's arm tighten, draw her that little bit closer, and
assumed he was guiding her away from a collision. But
glancing about she saw that no one else was near, there was
still plenty of room on the floor. She looked up then, and
met a warm look head-on.

'How beautiful you are,' he murmured.

Her throat felt choked. His words seemed as sincere as his
look. 'Thank you,' she said, and felt breathless. Then she
had to force herself to remember that there had been other
times when he had looked and sounded sincere.

'Can you, just for tonight, forget your low opinion of me?'
Nate asked, executing a neat corner, his hold on her
slackening not at all as he looked into her eyes.

Her heart pounding, Kathryn felt she should say, 'Why
should I?' but just then she was having difficulty in
remembering why it was she had a low opinion of him, or
indeed, if her opinion of him *was* low.

'I—wouldn't want to do anything that would upset your
uncle, tonight of all nights,' she compromised—and hoped,
since she could no longer be sure of the effect Nate was
having on her, that she wouldn't involuntarily be sending a
smile winging his way at some unguarded moment during
the evening, that if that happened he would believe she was
doing her best not to let hostility show purely for George's
sake.

Her remark seemed to be enough to satisfy Nate, although
he was unsmiling as he drew her that fraction closer,
causing her to hope he wouldn't ask her to dance again.
Though she wondered how she could wish to deny herself
when the music drew to a close and his head came forward
to the cap of her hair, a moment when his arm gripped
before he released his hold and stood back to thank her
before escorting her back to their table.

She met up with him again in a Paul Jones, and couldn't
help but laugh up at him when he outsmarted another man

when it looked as though he would claim her when the music stopped, the other man being the nearer of the two.

'Enjoying yourself?' he enquired, looking as though he was.

'I'm having a lovely time,' she said, because just then she couldn't be anything other than truthful.

Her answer had pleased him, she saw that in the smile that lit his eyes, warmed his mouth. And then the music had changed and they were separated again.

Kathryn continued to have a good time. She danced with all the Kingersby men in turn, even George got up with her to execute a version of the tango she was sure he had invented on the spot.

But it was as the band leader announced the last waltz that she caught Nate looking at her as though he was going to claim this dance as his, and panic set in. He would hold her close again, the lights would dim, and—and her resistance to him weakened and she had the most dreadful feeling she would again be making a fool of herself.

Nate stood up. And so did she. 'There's bound to be a fearful rush for coats,' she said to anyone who might be interested. 'I think I'll go now before the queue starts.' And without waiting for anyone to reply, she picked up her evening purse and was making for the cloakroom.

The queue had already started she discovered when she got there. So that by the time she had claimed her wrap, exchanged a remark here and there with some of her colleagues, it was to find the Kingersbys en masse in the foyer saying goodnight to people as they left.

'We're going back to my place for a nightcap,' George told her as he shook her hand. 'Will you join us, Kathryn?'

Overwhelmingly conscious of Nate nearby, she shook her head, smiling as she thanked him all the same, and quipping, 'Better not. I have to be up for work in the morning and my boss is a demon to work for!'

And stupidly, she thought later, she was afraid to even shake hands with Nate, knowing the evening had already weakened her too much where he was concerned; afraid just then that even the touch of his hand on her skin would have her eyes showing she had lost any semblance of coolness, so she included him in her goodnight to George and hurried out to find her car.

She had been driving for some fifteen minutes when she saw a car coming up behind her fast. Anticipating that it would overtake, flash past, she kept well over. But it didn't overtake. It slowed down to match her speed, turned when she turned, so that after first suspecting she was being tailed, she soon became certain that she was.

But by the time she drew the Mini up at her flat, she knew exactly who it was who was following her, and any apprehension she had felt at some stranger tailing her had gone. Only apprehension was in her heart that she still did not feel up to being cool with Nate Kingersby.

He was standing on the pavement waiting for her when she left her car. 'I thought it was you,' she said, powerless to snap at him.

'I didn't think you'd allow me to see you home,' he answered, letting her know he hadn't missed the way she had avoided having the last waltz with him, the way she had departed. 'But I hope you'll forgive me. You knew I wasn't happy about you risking that dynamo at this time of night.'

Standing with him, she couldn't deny a thrill that he felt the need to be protective. 'Well, I made it,' she said, not wanting to go in, having to force her feet away from him towards the direction of the front door. Her heart began acting up again as she found Nate had moved too—had moved, had taken charge of her hands, was preventing her from taking another step.

'Thank you for tonight,' he said quietly. 'Thank you for

helping to make this evening a night my uncle will remember only with happiness.' And while his touch was working that spell over her, he leaned forward and gently kissed her mouth. 'Goodnight, Kathryn,' he murmured, his voice thickened, and let go her hands.

'Goodnight,' she choked, and went indoors.

With daylight sanity returned, and with it the realisation that she still had over a week to go to work out her notice. Over a week, when the chilly front she had determined to show Nate already had gaping holes in it.

'Good morning, Kathryn,' he called pleasantly when she presented herself at the office.

'Good morning,' she replied stiffly, and if he had been about to spend a few minutes in general discussion on the success the celebration had been, then she didn't give him the chance as straightaway she got stuck into her work.

Time and time again that day, with Nate ignoring any ice directed at him, Kathryn had to put all her will to use not to melt. And never more so when she took in a letter from one of the files he had asked to see. He didn't offer to take the letter from her but was standing beside her checking the various points while she held the letter out, and it was when his hand hovered over hers as he pointed out the relevant part that her nerves betrayed her.

Her hand started to tremble that his hand might brush hers. Desperately striving for control, she saw that he could not help noticing how the paper she was holding was fluttering as if a breeze had taken it.

Without saying a word Nate took the letter from her and moved quickly to capture her trembling hand before, childishly, she would have put it behind her back.

'What's this?' he asked, oh, so softly, his eyes warm on her face.

Wanting to say something must be pressing on a nerve

but not having even that excuse since her arm had been free,
Kathryn stayed dumb, just staring at him, his hold on her
hand having her quivering inside.

What her eyes communicated to him she had no idea, but
suddenly his face was creasing into a smile. And while she
just stood there swallowing and fighting for control, Nate
brought her hand to his mouth and slowly kissed it.

Wild longings of wanting to throw herself into his arms
took her, but were instantly squashed as she made herself
remember that terrible disillusionment she had suffered at
his hands.

'Stop that!' she cried, snatching her hand out of his and
dreadfully afraid he would take hold of her hand again, that
she wouldn't have the strength to resist a second time,
bitterly she hurled at him, 'Isn't one seduction enough for
you?'

He didn't like being reminded, she could see that as his
face darkened. 'You're determined to disbelieve my motives,
aren't you?' he said shortly, thrusting his hands into his
pockets as if trying to overcome the way she fired his temper.
'Even though I can see you're not immune to me.'

'I have first-hand proof that your motives are more than
suspect,' she flung at him. And, unable to answer the charge
of not being immune to him tried to make out it wouldn't
bother her if she never saw him again, 'Roll on next Friday
when I shan't have to put up with you any more!'

It said a lot for Nate's self-control, she thought later, that
when it had looked as though he would really let fly, the
glint that came to his eyes telling her as much, he took a
deep breath, bit down whatever he had to say, and to her
amazement strode from the office.

But it was just after lunch the next afternoon that she had
a very definite feeling that she had pushed him too far. He
was on the point of leaving to spend the afternoon with
their biggest client. She knew his meeting would take all

afternoon and that he wouldn't be back before she went, and was looking at his bent head as she took a file of calculations in he wanted to take with him, when, nothing there for her to trip over, her eyes intent on him, her footing went astray and she would have gone flying had he not at that moment looked up, leapt from his chair and caught her.

For a moment she hadn't a clue what had happened, and just leaned weakly against him getting her bearings. And when she did fathom out that she was in his arms because she had tripped and he had moved quickly to save her, she still didn't have the sense to pull out of his arms.

'Did you hurt yourself?' Nate enquired above her head.

She looked up then, was pliant in his arms as she said, 'No, I'm all right.'

His blue eyes took on warmth, went from the wide brown velvet of hers, to move to her slightly parted mouth. 'Good,' he said softly, and then heaven was hers as his head came down, his hold tightening as his mouth covered hers.

Kathryn returned his kiss simply because she felt starved of his kisses. Her arms went up and around him in a mindless world where nothing else mattered as his kiss deepened, he pressed her to him, and drew the very soul from her.

But it was Nate who was first to draw back, loosening his grip on her a little as he leaned away, a smile ready to break, she was sure, as he looked into her eyes. Then very softly he was saying:

'My timing was all wrong before.' And while she hadn't an earthly what he meant, suddenly there was no smile in him, only seriousness the longer he looked at her, and then he said, 'Tell me now, Kathryn—are you going to marry me?'

Pink colour flooded her face as her heart pumped madly and the word yes trembled on her lips. And then those nightmare remembrances were with her again, remembrances of how she had thought he had meant she should be his wife once before—a voice of truth taunting, you've been fooled by him before—and it steadied her, had her doing then what she should have done minutes ago.

She pulled out of his arms, saw he was still unsmiling as his brow came down at her action, then found that weak though his touch, his kiss, had made her, she still had pride enough, strength enough to reject him.

'Still suffering from a guilty conscience, Nate?' she derided, and regardless of the way his eyes narrowed at her tone, went on whipping herself into squaring up to him— that or give in. 'And there was I thinking you were too much a man of the world to lose any sleep over the fact that you took some poor little nonentity's virginity!'

This time, as he hung on to the temper she could see her taunts had stirred, Nate did not go storming out, and she just had to admire the way he stuck it out and asked for more when he grated:

'Are you? Tell me yes or no. Are you going to marry me?'

'What?' She found a note of mockery to help her. 'You'd have me say yes? You must think I was born yesterday!' And mockery left, truth alone coming from her with the tortured words, 'You think I'd trust you again after what you did? You think I'd ever say yes? That I would go to the church only to find I'd been left at the altar—It's what you planned for me, isn't it?'

She had given him his answer, told him as clearly as she could that under no circumstances would she trust him not to let her down, that whatever motives he had for asking her to marry him, whether they be in recompense for what he had done or if his motive was still that he was out to avenge Rex, then in neither case would she take the risk of arriving for a marriage ceremony only to find no groom waiting for her.

From the firmness of his jaw, from the tight line of his mouth, she saw he had controlled his anger. But it was seconds before he spoke, and what he said then had her disintegrating.

'I deserve your wrath—more possibly considering the harm I meant you,' he said tautly. 'I deserve too that you have little trust in me.' And there was that in his look as his blue eyes refused to let her brown ones look away that had any mockery and derision in her a thing of the past, as, his voice suddenly deadly quiet, he said, 'But just answer me one question.' And while she waited, knowing from his quietly determined look that she didn't want to hear his question, much less answer it, he floored her by saying, 'You once declared that you loved me. Have I by my actions killed that love? Or do you love me still?'

Tears sprang to Kathryn's eyes as she tried to find words to deny that love, tears she couldn't hope to hide, tears that try as hard as she might she could not oust the love she had for Nate. It would survive no matter what he did.

Frantically she tried to swallow her tears, saw him move and knew he had read his answer. And because she knew what his touch could do to her, his movement had her hastily backing away. 'Oh, for God's sake!' rang from her, and then she was racing for the cloakroom.

Ten minutes later, torn between the desire to go home, forget all about coming to work next week, she felt her duty as secretary to the chairman catch at her desire to run away and hide. And pride was there again, pride that said she had a job to do.

Sure in her mind that Nate had left for his appointment, Kathryn came out of the cloakroom. He would be late for his meeting if he hadn't gone, she thought, and he was too much of a business man to risk offending their client. By Monday she would be more up to seeing him again.

But to her consternation, she found that Nate hadn't gone. He was still in his office, the briefcase in his hand telling her he was on the point of leaving. But, more in control now than when she had run for the cloakroom, she still had no intention of meeting his eyes.

That was until he came striding purposely through. He came from his office and halted by her desk, and she had to look up then in case he wanted to give her some instructions.

Brown eyes clashed mutinously with steady, iron-determined blue ones—Kathryn's eyes the first to falter. For Nate was looking at her as if to say that because of what he had done he had let her get away with murder. But now, having his offer of marriage refused for a second time, he was not prepared to put up with her vilification a moment longer.

She was sure of it when after tense seconds she heard him move, heard the door close quietly behind him, and realised that without saying a word, silently, he had gone off to keep his appointment.

Nothing had come from him in the way of a goodbye, no comment whatsoever that her eyes were still tinged red from the tears she hadn't been able to hold back in the cloakroom. And had it been all her highly pitched awareness of him that had had her thinking that Nate Kingersby had been pushed too far?

She had to wait until Monday to find out. But she felt herself tremble that his look, if her imagination hadn't gone completely wild, had certainly said he had decided on some course of action where she was concerned.

CHAPTER TEN

As she left home earlier than usual on Monday, knowing she had a five-minute walk to the office after she had left her car at the garage, Kathryn had very mixed feelings about the coming week.

Not for the first time did she wonder, as she had on many occasions over the weekend, why she hadn't said yes when Nate had asked if she was going to marry him. Had she agreed, she thought yet again, then there would be no need to say goodbye to him this Friday.

She was still at war with herself at the thought of what a fool she had been not to jump at the chance to share her life with him when she drove into the garage and handed over her car keys, and pondered again on what was in her that made her refuse what the gods were offering.

But deep down she knew what it was that prevented her from risking that Nate still might have plans to leave her, in the words of the old song, 'waiting at the church'. She knew what it was that even if he wasn't still set on punishing her for being indirectly responsible for Rex's accident had made her refuse. Nate had made no mention of the word love in his proposal. He did not love her. And that was at the root of it.

How could she marry a man whose only reason for saying he would marry her was some quixotic gesture? If what he said was true, that a Kingersby fell in love only once, and for ever—and that must mean Rex had never truly loved her—then how could she marry Nate only to fear every day that he might have met some other woman and found that once-in-a-lifetime love? She didn't have to look beyond his

171

marriage proposal to know his honour would have him staying married to her. What sort of a marriage would that be, with him yearning to be with another woman?

Still trying to convince herself she had been right to turn him down, Kathryn entered her office remembering, as she had a dozen or more times over the weekend, the impression she had received on Friday that she had pushed Nate too far. The impression that he had taken the gloves off and that just one step out of line and she would find she was being sorted out in no uncertain terms.

But as she greeted him with a civil, 'Good morning,' and received his cool, positively remote response, her brow wrinkled. He had met her civility with none of the aggression she had expected. Perhaps it *had* been imagination pure and simple that had led her to believe he had taken all he intended taking from her, that he had decided on a way to deal with her!

But she was wary of him. No sign of his aggression so far anyway, she thought as she sat with her ankles neatly crossed, taking down his lengthy dictation. But there was something different about him this morning. Some—what it was she couldn't quite pinpoint. He had always been assertive, but this morning there seemed to be an added assertiveness about him, a sort of positiveness that told her he was a man who knew what he wanted, a man who had decided what he wanted and had made up his mind to go out and get it.

And that didn't make sense either, for when, dictation finished, she went to rise, he stayed her by remarking, still in that same cool, remote voice he had used from the time she had gone in:

'I want everything cleared up before the weekend.' And not because he wouldn't have her as his secretary next Monday, she soon discovered when he unbent sufficiently to explain, 'I'm taking two weeks' holiday.'

'Holiday?' Kathryn couldn't help the exclamation, and saw his look become arrogant as if he didn't care much that she might be thinking he shouldn't at this particular time.

'If you have no objection,' he remarked sarcastically, and not waiting for her to bite, went on, 'My uncle will stand in for me from Monday onwards.'

'B-But he won't have a secretary,' she said, forgetting his sarcasm while she wondered if he was leading up to ask her if she would stay on another two weeks—for all the indifferent way he was talking to her wasn't the manner of a man about to ask favours.

'Of course, you're leaving on Friday, aren't you,' he said, as if it was so unimportant it had needed her reminder to prompt the memory. And far from asking her to stay on, he didn't seem to think her efficiency as a secretary was anything out of the way. 'Well, I don't doubt we'll be able to rope in a girl from one of the other offices.'

Kathryn firmed her mouth. She would have got up then and gone back to her desk, hiding her hurt, but Nate hadn't finished yet.

'I shall be out for the next hour or so,' he told her, making her blink, because there was nothing in his appointment book for this morning.

She almost said so, but bit the words back as she realised he was probably popping out to make his holiday arrangements. Though knowing him she would have thought he would have got her to do it for him, or have phoned, rather than waste his valuable time on a personal visit.

'You've got enough to keep you busy until I get back?' he enquired coolly, which annoyed her because he should know her well enough by now to know that if she hadn't she would find something. Apart from the fact that he must know he had given her enough dictation to keep her busy until lunchtime.

'Yes, I think so,' she replied, trying to keep her voice even, but aware as he must be there that was a tinge of sarcasm in her answer.

'Good,' he said, taking her remark at face value apparently. He then consulted his watch and stood up, about to leave his office, then suddenly he remembered something and stayed to dip his hand into his inside pocket. 'My brother asked me to give you this,' he said. And while Kathryn sat and stared at him wide-eyed, he handed her a letter.

'From Rex?' she exclaimed without thought.

'Rex is the only brother I have,' he replied loftily, which niggled her again, so that at that moment she wanted nothing to do with either brother, and could just as easily consigned the letter unread into the paper basket.

Then she found Nate had seen what was going through her mind, when curtly he told her, 'I'd advise you to read it first before you throw it away.'

'You know what he's written!' she exclaimed, certain from his remark that he must.

'As a matter of fact, yes,' he replied, and without another word left for wherever it was he was going.

For several minutes after the outer door had closed, she did not move; Nate's attitude had given her plenty to think about. She couldn't help but remember back to Friday, or to reflect that with the way he was being today, if he considered she had been compromised half a dozen times over, then never again would he ask 'Are you going to marry me?'

And so much for her thinking he was being more assertive than usual! The assertive manner was there, undoubtedly, but what sort of head of company was it who decided he intended to go out and get whatever it was he was being particularly assertive about, by going on holiday?

Jealousy picked at her that he was going on holiday with some woman he knew, and she couldn't take it. Needing action, she leaned forward, took hold of his paper knife and slit open the envelope he had handed her, wondering sourly why it was sealed at all since Nate knew what Rex had written. A minute later, so did she.

'Dear Kathryn,' Rex had written, 'If you have got this far without tearing up any communication from me, then may I hope you don't hate me as much as I deserve?

To apologise for the terrible shock you received that awful day isn't sufficient, but I do humbly ask you to forgive the hurt I caused you.

Lying here has given me plenty of time to think. Time to realise that while you are more special than at the time we were engaged I was able to see that the love we shared was not the love that true, everlasting marriages are made of. How otherwise could I have done what I did? How else could you keep away from the hospital?

There will always be a deep affection in my heart for you, Kathryn. Be happy, darling. Love, Rex.'

'Oh, Rex!' Kathryn whispered softly, and remembering all the good times they had shared, felt an affection stir in her heart too. She was glad he had seen they hadn't loved each other the way they should have done. She saw then what their relationship had been all about—it had been a skirmish into romance, possibly something that had to happen so that when real love came along they would both recognise it. One day Rex would find himself everlastingly in love, the way Nate had said Kingersbys gave their hearts only once. The way she, who was not a Kingersby, had given her heart. All she hoped was that when the time came for Rex to bestow his heart, he fared better with his love than she had.

'Read your letter?' was the first thing Nate asked when he came striding in nearly two hours later.

'Yes,' she replied. And since he seemed to be waiting for more she found some coolness of her own when she said, 'I won't bother you with my reply—I'll post it.'

'Does the fact that you're answering it at all mean you're prepared to forgive him?' he asked abruptly.

And her coolness evaporated then, because that could only mean Nate's love for his brother had him wanting to protect Rex if she intended writing anything that would upset him.

'Yes,' she replied quietly. 'I—I find I still feel an affection for him.'

'But you don't love him?' The question came aggressively, and with the same rapidity as a rocket-projected missile.

Sorely tempted to say she did love Rex, reasoning that it might take any idea out of Nate's head that she might love him, she took her time in answering, which didn't suit him at all.

'Well?' he rapped impatiently. And looking at him, she just couldn't voice the lie.

'I believe I told you once before that I no longer love him,' she said, and analysing what she did feel for Rex, she shrugged and explained, 'My feelings for him are—sisterly, I suppose.'

To her surprise, and had she not been looking at him she would have missed it, she could have sworn Nate's face took on a look of such instantaneous delight, for all it was quickly concealed, that it baffled her. But the change in his expression had been fleeting, quickly banished, and could never have been she thought, as straight away his face became stern and arrogant.

'Have you typed that dictation back yet?' he asked shortly, making her want to hit him suddenly, because fast she was, but not jet-engined.

On Friday morning she rose early, looked at the suit she intended to wear that day, a suit Nate had seen her in several times, and suddenly she wanted to wear something more eye-catching than that.

It was perverse of her to want to catch his attention, she knew that, when all week she had taken her impersonal attitude from him. Not once had he smiled at her. He had kept up that cool remoteness just as though he couldn't wait for today to end and with it her job with the company. Not once had she caught his eyes staring at her mouth as sometimes they had, staring as if he was remembering the kisses they had exchanged.

But having told herself the week had progressed as she wanted it, purely secretary and boss, no warmth emitted from either side, she found as she looked distastefully at the suit she was to put on that she wanted Nate to treat her differently from the robot she was sure was what he had seen her as ever since Monday morning.

She took a peep out of the window. It looked like being a beautiful day out there. And it was the weather that decided her on the blue crêpey dress that was a shade dressy for the office, but acceptable.

Having washed her hair last night, although Thursday wasn't a regular hair-washing night, she sat before her dressing table mirror-brushing the shining cap around her ears, and was glad she had done so. And when she was ready at last she couldn't help the thought, as she looked at her reflection, that if she didn't get at least a tiny reaction, then she would know a robot was all Nate Kingersby considered her.

But if she had made an extra effort that morning, then Nate, who was in her office when she went in, was more immaculate than she had ever seen him. He was wearing a dark suit she had never seen before, and where she couldn't remember him wearing at work anything but coloured shirts, or a white shirt with a stripe in it, this morning he was wearing the crispest white shirt she had ever seen. His shoes too looked as though they had received an extra rub, even his thick dark hair looked as though he had tried to

tame it with a brush. The whole effect of him made her
heart turn over, he looked so superb.

'G-Good morning,' Kathryn managed, trying to tear her
eyes away.

'Good morning,' he replied. And it was there, the admiration her foolish heart wanted, there in his eyes as they swept
from her shining head to her dainty shoes. 'May I say
you're looking particularly lovely this morning?' he added.

But the glow that had warmed her had her feeling less of a
robot, vanished abruptly when at ten o'clock Nate told her
he was going out. And she was absolutely devastated that
he could be so uncaring as to add, as if by the way, that he
wouldn't be back that day.

'I might as well say goodbye now,' she said, striving not to
cry, because it looked as if his head was so full of the
holiday he was going on, he had forgotten this was her last
day.

Pride would still have had her holding out her hand if he
had, but he didn't. He merely looked at her as though he
had a hundred and one things to sort out about his holiday,
while she was just another secretary on her way out.

'*Au revoir*,' was all he said, and went quickly, avoiding the
hurt in her eyes.

Kathryn tried to rail against him when he had gone. She
needed that anger; tried to scorn his *Au revoir* when he
knew very well they wouldn't be seeing each other again.
But she felt so heartsore she wasn't at all certain she was
going to keep her tears down for very much longer.

The way Nate had so casually parted from her after all
that lay between them was still occupying all her thoughts
when just before eleven the phone rang, and she almost
had heart failure to hear his voice ordering:

'Pack up and leave whatever you're in the middle of,
Kathryn. Come and have a farewell drink with me.'

'I . . .'

That was as far as she managed, her wits scattered to hear his voice so unexpectedly. Belatedly the thought came that it was usual to have a farewell lunchtime session on one's last day, although it was nowhere near lunch time. But she had done nothing about telling anyone else she was leaving, nor for that matter had she done anything about organising a get-together in the pub across the road.

'Did you hear me, Kathryn?'

'We've said our goodbyes,' she said, not wanting another casual *Au revoir*, although she was aching for one last chance to see him.

And then there was a change in Nate when his voice came again. He wasn't ordering her this time. A coaxing note was there that had her backbone turning to water.

'Would you disappoint your fellow workers just because you've seen enough of me?' he asked softly.

Her resistance was rapidly disappearing. She had to fasten on to something. 'Fellow workers?' she queried, and joy burst senselessly in her heart that he couldn't have meant her to leave without some sort of send-off. 'Have you arranged for people I know to be there?'

'I assure you, you'll soon be seeing a whole host of people you know,' he thrilled her by saying.

Bearing in mind that they worked flexi-time, that lunchtime was staggered between twelve and two, Kathryn saw she would have to be there at twelve to greet the first arrivals.

'I'll leave about five to twelve.' She gave in, simply because she wanted to.

'Leave now, Kathryn. We're not using the pub across the road.'

'But we always use the Crown for . . .' she started to say— only to be informed that they weren't today, as Nate mentioned a plushy hotel she would need to take her car to get to.

'Come now,' he ended, and was so commanding again as he put down the phone that she knew he would be angry if she disobeyed him.

She looked down at the matter in her typewriter. She had an urge brought about by the efficiency in her secretarial soul to stay and finish it, but was then swamped by an even bigger urge to see Nate as soon as possible. He had ordered her to 'Come now', after all, hadn't he? she quietened her secretary's conscience as she pulled the paper out of her machine and stuffed it away in a drawer.

Then she was in the cloakroom, washing her hands, tidying her hair, checking on her make-up, before going out to the car park.

At a quarter past eleven she was slowing down her Mini and looking for a place to park. The hotel was to her left, but a drayman's lorry was blocking up the entrance to the rear. She spotted a place near a church opposite just about right for her small car, she thought, and was in there with a nifty piece of parking while her heartbeats were telling her, for all she might look cool, it had recognised the excitement with which she was anticipating meeting Nate on the semi-business, semi-social occasion.

Locking the car, she turned and crossed the road, then composing her features she mounted the steps to the hotel. Pushing through the revolving door, she saw Nate at once standing there waiting for her, looking more dashing than she had ever seen him, his immaculate appearance added to in the shape of a red rose attached to the lapel of his jacket.

He smiled, and she didn't know if it was because he was pleased to see her, but thought it more probably because she had obeyed his instructions.

'Come with me,' he said, barely greeting her as he took hold of her arm and escorted her into some sort of an anteroom.

It passed through her mind to think it was going to be a

bit of a crush if all her colleagues assembled in this room. For apart from a two-seater settee and an easy chair, there was no other seating accommodation, and only one very small occasional table. Still, if Nate had arranged with the management that they use this room, having no argument with the smartness of the place, then most of them would have to stand and hold their drinks.

Nate closed the door and led her straight to the settee, then sat down with her, surprising her, for although she wasn't particularly bothered about a drink, she would have thought he would have gone to the bar or have rung for service.

Tension then became a tight knot inside her to have him sitting so close. The earliest anyone else could get here would be another hour's time. Oh, why had she rushed to do his bidding?

'Do you—er—think there's room for them all in here?' came blurting from her, conscious as she was that he had turned and was looking at her. 'It—er—might be a bit of a crush—don't you think?'

'It would be,' Nate agreed solemnly, too close for comfort, and to her astonishment, 'if we were expecting anyone else to turn up here.'

'Not exp . . .!' Her eyes flew to his, her surprise not diminished when fresh shock hit her that never had she seen Nate looking more purposeful. 'What—do you mean?' she gasped. 'On the phone you said . . .'

'Forget for a moment what I told you over the phone, Kathryn, and listen to what I have to say now.'

'But . . .' She struggled with something not unlike fear, for the seriousness of his expression told her he had something of vital importance to say. But she was unable to forget he had got her there on the pretence that a whole crowd of people would be there, and yet here he was now saying . . .

Shock, fear, tension, all emotions went save the anger that replaced them. 'You think you'll stand less chance of us being disturbed if you give me the dressing down you think I deserve here for my not being a meek and mild secretary,' she challenged. The way he had looked at her last Friday shot into her head, that look that had said he intended to deal with her in his own way, and suddenly she was convinced that was why he had got her there.

But instead of starting to sort her out, Nate looked back at her, not a glimmer of a smile anywhere about him. 'You don't trust me an inch, do you?'

'No, I don't,' she fired back.

'Have you never fully believed how sincerely I regret the way we started out? Have you never believed how bitter the taste of remorse has been for me to swallow?'

Anger cooled as quickly as it had come. Did she not believe that? How could she not, when the very fact that he had twice intimated he would marry her told her how that word 'honour' rested with him?

'Y-Yes,' she said slowly, not wanting to. A feeling came over her that since they were to part, loving him as she did, how could she bear that he should not know himself believed? 'Yes, I believe you,' she added, her voice very low.

A slight easing came to his expression at that, but his face was still unsmiling when he said, 'You found it in your heart to forgive my brother, Kathryn. My crime—the sin I committed against you was far greater.' He took hold of her hand, his touch burning although his hand was cool. 'Can you find room in your heart to try to forgive me?' he asked, his sincerity without question.

Kathryn wanted to say 'Why should I?' but they had been over all that before. And with his deep regret, his sincere wish that she try to forgive him, and with his hand now gripping hers, she just couldn't find any hate in her with which to revile him. And suddenly, looking into those earnest blue eyes, she could find no bitterness in her with which to rail against him either. What he had done he had done because of love for a brother he thought she had broken.

'Oh, Nate,' she said, and saw then why he had brought her away from the office. This matter was a personal one—personal to Nate and her. He had wanted to have her forgiveness before she said goodbye to him for ever. That thought alone, that this time her goodbye to him would be final, had her battling desperately so he shouldn't see she was falling apart inside, had her exerting what will power she had to find some stiffening. She mustn't go weak at the knees just because he was holding her hand while waiting for her to add something to that 'Oh, Nate' that had left her. She must tell him she forgave him in an adult way, must shake hands and then go. She dredged up a surface smile. 'Life's too short to go around bearing a grudge, isn't it?' she succeeded in saying lightly.

But as her light tone reached him she saw at once from the pulse that beat in his temple that he just wasn't believing she didn't hold the past against him. Then even instinct was working against her, her heart stronger than her head, so that without her knowing it her hand was gripping his in return, and she could be no other than natural with him. She could not beat down that part of her that had the sincerity of her feelings coming through, that had her speaking softly:

'I forgive you, Nate, of course I do.' And as a light showed in his eyes how much her forgiveness meant to him, to his honour she had to remind herself, she smiled a natural smile, and told him, 'I'm glad you arranged this meeting. It's easier to talk here than in the office, isn't it? A-And I shouldn't like to have left with things—the way they were.'

'Kathryn—my dear!' The tenderness in Nate's voice had

her bones ready to melt even before he added, 'The sweetness of you makes me more aware than ever of how deeply I've wronged you.' Then, his voice stronger, 'I shall work on getting you to trust me completely. But for the moment, will you try to trust me just a little?'

Knowing herself confused, for very soon she would be walking away from him, away from any chance of learning to trust, she looked at him blankly. Then she knew he had seen she was lost to what he was talking about, and tried desperately hard to keep her emotions under control when he raised her hand to his lips and kissed it, his eyes holding hers.

'You once told me in no uncertain terms, did you not, that you wouldn't marry me because you had little faith that I wouldn't leave you humiliated in front of the wedding guests by not turning up?' he asked, setting her heart banging against her ribs that he should suddenly switch the conversation back to the one of marriage.

'Yes,' she said, her voice barely audible as it came to her to wonder if he intended a last try to fully redeem his honour by asking her a third time to marry him. And to wonder if, with Nate still holding on to her hand, no animosity between them now, she would have the strength to say no!

'Then,' he said, his eyes positively burning into hers, some emotion there she couldn't recognise, 'since both you and I are here, our relatives and friends assembled over the road, will you, Kathryn, give me that little trust I ask for and come across the road with me?'

'Across the road with you?' she choked, trying to take in what he had said, that friends *and relatives* were across the road. And recalling she had parked her car across the road, across the road by the . . . 'But it's a—a church over there,' came croakily from her.

'It is,' he agreed, taking in the shock that took her, his

voice gentle as he went on, 'Whether you come with me or
not, Kathryn—and from the bottom of my heart I hope you
will—I shall have to go. But I hope very much I shall not
have to go and explain that my bride has decided to leave
me at the altar.'

'Bride?' Stunned, Kathryn was capable only of staring at
him.

'I have a special licence all ready,' he said. 'The ceremony
is set for twelve o'clock.' And, never more sincere, 'If you
want retribution for all the harm I've done you, Kathryn,
you have it at your disposal.'

Witlessly she gaped at him. The words, bride, special
licence, twelve o'clock, were enough to have her brain
patterns chaotic. That Nate had got all that arranged—
their marriage—winded her so that she was capable only of
sitting and staring, until what else he had said started to
filter through the gamut of her thoughts.

'You mean . . .' she groped, fastening on the word
retribution as her intelligence righted itself, 'You mean I
could—that if . . .' It was all too much, but Nate was allowing her all the time she needed to give him her answer. 'You
mean I could have my—retribution by—letting you go
across to that ch-church by yourself . . .? That y-you'd sink
your pride and allow me to—do that to you?'

'I would,' he answered solemnly.

But still her mind reeled. He had arranged for them to be
married—now! But why? Even knowing how truly sorry he
was for what he had done, she still couldn't take it in. That
he meant what he said she couldn't doubt, but surely—he
wouldn't have gone this far just for the sake of honour? Just
for the sake of allowing her to score off him.

'Why, Nate?' she asked, her voice becoming clearer as
shock receded, 'It—It isn't just because you want to show
me true remorse, is it?'

Slowly he shook his head. 'No, it isn't,' he agreed. Then

his eyes left hers as he took a moment out to consult his watch.

Kathryn followed his action. She saw for herself that minute hand was ticking steadily towards noon, but still she needed the answer to her question.

'I was hoping to save the explanation for later,' Nate said, his eyes once more intent on hers. 'But I've wounded your trust too badly to expect you to come with me without question, haven't I?'

The love she had for him would have had her going anywhere with him, but she couldn't deny that what he had done to her had not left her trust in him unaffected. And Nate seemed then not to need to have his question answered, for he was all understanding as he took up many more precious minutes as he started to explain, by beginning:

'You too mentioned the word remorse. Remorse—contrition, I've been awash with it, am going to be plagued by it for a long time to come.' He smiled then as if to soften his next words. 'But by the end of last week I felt it was all used up. I'd put up with more from you than I thought I would ever put up with from any woman. But because I knew better than anyone the good reason you had, I've taken it—taken it when a time or two you have had me so furious I came near to the edge of blasting you.'

Kathryn knew he was speaking the truth. She could clearly remember that day he had slammed back to his own office when it had looked as though he was about to explode and start slamming into her. And remembering some of the stinging remarks she had hurled at him, she couldn't help feeling a tinge of remorse herself.

'Then last Friday,' he continued when he could see this was one time when she had nothing to come back with, 'last Friday when I asked you if I'd killed the love you once said you had for me . . .'

She tried to pull her hand from his, wanted to run from

him. But he wouldn't let her. He held firmly on to her hand, gathering up the other one so she was securely tethered, no chance of escape.

'. . . and I saw the answer there in your eyes. I knew you still felt the same way about me in spite of all I'd done. I knew it even before you came back and your eyes showed you'd been weeping. I knew then that if we were ever to get anywhere I should have to do something constructive about it.'

Kathryn couldn't look at him any longer. Wrenching her eyes away, she stared numbly down at their hands. She had never felt so dreadful in her life as she drew on the little pride he had left her with.

'You don't—you don't have to marry me just because you've found out I—care,' she said woodenly.

And she knew she was going to come out of this second best when Nate let go one of her hands, ending any hope for clear thinking with what tattered remains she had left by putting his arm around her shoulders, pulling her close as he let go her other hand and placed his hand under her chin to tilt up her face. Then looking deeply into her eyes, eyes that couldn't escape him, he smiled. Then he was dipping his head to kiss her lips in a slow gentle benediction.

'My darling Kathryn,' he murmured, his voice full of emotion, his eyes holding hers again, 'Don't you know yet that part of the reason I've taken all you've thrown at me is because I care for you too?'

'You—care for me!' she echoed incredulously, her eyes flying wide.

'To be more precise, my dearest one,' said Nate, his tones tender, his voice thickening, 'I love you to distraction. I've known myself in love with you since that moment you arrived at my home in Surrey.'

'You can't be in l-love with me?' She couldn't believe it. 'You were horrible to me—to begin with,' she remembered, a pink she couldn't hope to avoid colouring her skin at her memories of afterwards.

'Believe me, my only love,' Nate told her gently, 'it was only because I had at that moment recognised what the unwanted attraction I felt for you was that I started out by being vile to you that day.'

'You—you've been attracted to me?' she asked, still unable to believe any of this was happening. Had Nate really said he loved her?

'Almost from the first,' he confirmed. 'Though because of what I thought you'd done to my brother I turned my back on it, fought against the attraction of you. I didn't want anything to detract me from the iniquitous course I'd plotted for you.'

'That's why you were horrible to me at your home—t-to start with, because of your—plan?' she asked, puzzled because if he had carried on being the way he had started out by being, she would not have stayed the night—nothing would have hap . . .

'I'd just realised I was in love with you. My plans were all over the place as we worked on. I was too busy trying to come to terms with my stupidity, asking myself how could I have allowed myself to fall for the woman I then thought you to be. You jerked me out of my thoughts by looking as though you were going to cry, and I had a few short moments of heaven just holding you in my arms. And then thoughts of Rex were intruding again. I had to force myself to remember him—his pain. It became easier then to remember the revenge I thought you deserved.'

His voice faded, but the grip he had of her, his arm across her shoulders tightening, the look on his face, all showed her he was trying to get on top as remembrance of what had followed smote him. And Kathryn just knew then that he was thinking of the way she had so willingly given herself to him.

'Oh, my dear love,' he said, swallowing hard as he overcame his emotion, 'you'll never know the tumult in me when I discovered that not only had you not been with my brother, but that no other man had known you. The torment that left me ragged had me leaving you at dawn. My brain was whirling with you, with Rex whose word I knew I could trust above any man's, but who had lied by leading me purposely to believe you and he had been lovers. I was nowhere near to sorting myself out when I heard you say "Hello, darling". I turned, saw you, knew the unpardonable wrong I'd done you, and while I still can't believe it myself, tried to find release from the terrible burden of guilt weighing me down by verbally attacking you.'

Kathryn knew she would never forget that time when her world had turned upside down. But looking at Nate she saw if it had dogged her heels then she hadn't been alone in her suffering, for his face had a haunted look to it as he too remembered and went on.

'Then you told me you loved me, told me the truth of your broken engagement; doing nothing to lessen the guilt that was in me—guilt that was crucifying me that two Kingersbys had abominably treated you, abused your love—and I just couldn't take it. I had to get out, had to go and try to clear my spinning head.'

Whether he saw in her eyes that his agony of mind was painful to her, she didn't know. But suddenly that haunted expression eased from him and in its place a smile started to grow, a smile that forced its way through and came from the very heart of him. A smile that warmed her through and through, so that she just had to smile back. She had to begin to trust, to begin to believe this wonderful thing he had said was true. That he was—in love with *her*.

'I don't think I was out for very long,' he said, his face coming nearer. 'I have little recollection of whether it was a few minutes or an hour. But by the time I went hurrying back to the house, I knew I'd lost all chance with you.'

'But you still tried,' she whispered huskily.

And at the way she was looking at him Nate seemed unable to say another word until he had savoured the sweetness of her mouth. It was a warm, gentle kiss, but even so it set her senses clamouring before he pulled back to look into her eyes.

'I wanted you so badly, Kathryn, love you so much, I just couldn't give you up without fighting for you.' He kissed her gently once more as if afraid to let himself go, then pulled back, his eyes full of love for her. 'Say again those words I'm longing to hear my beloved one,' he urged. 'Those words that mean you more than just *care* for me.'

'Oh, Nate!' Kathryn cried, her heart full, the look in his eyes, everything about him telling her she could trust him, that he did love her. 'Oh, Nate, I do love you so!'

Regardless of the minutes ticking away Nate just had to kiss her again, fold her in his arms and kiss her waiting mouth, her eyes, her face, hold her wrapped in his arms as though he never wanted to let her go.

But at last he drew back, drank in her love shining like a beacon from her eyes, and just had to kiss her again before memory stirred that they should by now be over at the church.

'I love you so, my dear love,' he said, his hands cupping her face. And, his expression at that moment totally serious, 'Will you cross the road with me? Will you, Kathryn, will you be my wife?'

'Yes, Nate—yes, I will,' she told him without hesitation, her own expression just as serious, until she saw the joyous smile that broke from him.

And then he was drawing her to her feet, removing the red rose from his lapel, pinning it on to her dress, just the touch from the backs of his fingers making her skin tingle.

'There'll be a bower of flowers waiting for you when we

get to Surrey,' he told her when the single red rose transferred from him to her was enough to have tears misting her eyes.

Then, taking time for one last kiss, Nate placed his arm securely round her and hugging her to him, careless that anyone seeing them as they crossed the road would know he adored her. He told her in the few minutes they had left that after the ceremony there was to be a reception at his uncle's home.

'Not your home?' she asked, uncaring of anything but the possessive way Nate's arm was about her.

'Too far,' he said, and looking deep into her eyes. 'Besides, I don't want anyone outstaying their welcome.' And, his eyes positively roguish, 'We'll need to have an early night since we're flying off early tomorrow.'

'Your holiday!' Kathryn suddenly remembered.

'Our honeymoon,' Nate corrected.

And they were at the church door, Nate firmly tucking her hand into his arm, his face sober now as together they walked down the aisle, faces familiar smiling at them—friends, Kingersbys, and in the front left-hand pew, Sandra, Vic and their two daughters.

Her quick look at Nate showed Kathryn he had read the question in her eyes of how had they got there. Then everything else was forgotten except that beautiful moment when she and Nate stood before the minister, Nate's voice firm as he vowed his undying love.

The wedding ring he slipped over her marriage finger fitted perfectly. Then before them all, as if he had forgotten the existence of the congregation, of anyone save her, Nate turned to look at her. And it was just as if he could not help himself, that vow of undying love still there in his eyes, that he gently gathered her into his arms.

'Will you trust me now, darling wife?' he whispered.

'I will, Nate,' she re-avowed, oblivious to anyone save him. 'I do.'

Harlequin Plus

A ROMANCE
THAT ROCKED THE WORLD

"You must believe me when I tell you that I have found it impossible to carry the heavy duty of responsibility and discharge my duties as King as I would wish to do, without the help and support of the woman I love. I now quit altogether public affairs and I lay down my burden."

There are many of us who recognize this famous speech. For with these words, broadcast to an astonished nation on December 11, 1936, King Edward VIII of Britain gave up his throne; he then traveled to France to marry the beautiful Wallis Warfield Simpson, a twice-divorced American whom the English Cabinet would not tolerate wed to their King. Little wonder that this love affair between the Duke of Windsor (the title Edward was later given) and Wallis Simpson has probably been the most talked about in the twentieth century!